"Will you come home with me tonight?"

Michael tightened his arms around her waist.

Megan tried to focus on the other dancers moving sinuously around them, but that did more harm than good. She looked up at the sparks of light bouncing off the mirrored globe, but they were too much like the sparks showering through her body. It was no use. The more she resisted the heat, the hotter the flames grew.

"Megan, I promise I'll answer all of your questions . . . but not tonight. Tonight, I don't want to talk at all."

Megan moaned softly as his mouth covered hers. She was flesh and blood and emotion, and so was Michael. In the morning she would tell him the truth. For now, *this* was what she wanted.

Michael cursed against her lips as he lowered his hand from her waist, his fingers boldly stroking down her hips and thigh.

"Say yes," he said huskily. "Or I swear I'll take you here and now, before God *and* the Righteous Brothers."

"Yes," she gasped. "Yes, Michael. Yes."

Marsha M. Canham is a bestselling historical romance author. This is her first foray into contemporary romance. With just the suggestion of "dark and dangerous," she wrote a suspenseful, sexy story. Marsha's wicked sense of humor always shows up in her delightful and bizarre characters—and often in real life. Long before she ever published with Harlequin, she teasingly picked out her pseudonym, Constance Fairbreast. She liked the name so much, you'll find it inside....

Marsha, her husband and their son make their home in Ontario, Canada.

Dark & Dangerous

MARSHA M. CANHAM

Harlequin Books

TORONTO • NEW YORK • LONDON
AMSTERDAM • PARIS • SYDNEY • HAMBURG
STOCKHOLM • ATHENS • TOKYO • MILAN
MADRID • WARSAW • BUDAPEST • AUCKLAND

To Brain Kelly,
for his sound advice, which I foolishly ignored until now

Published March 1992

ISBN 0-373-25486-5

DARK & DANGEROUS

Prologue

"I AM NOT a detective. I have no desire to be a detective, nor have I ever harbored aspirations of playing the part of the femme fatale in a spy novel. Most especially, I have no intentions of ruining my well-deserved vacation at the whim of a couple of white-collar flatfoots."

District Attorney Philip Levy leaned back in his chair and rubbed his hand wearily across his forehead. A gruff, gravel-voiced man who had won his appointment to office on a platform of tough justice, Phil was showing signs of strain from having to limit his use of four-letter expletives. Seated across from him, looking leggy and elegant in a tailored linen suit, was one of his assistant district attorneys, Megan Worth. What was saving her from a display of his infamous temper was that she was one of his best A.D.A.'s. That and the fact that he heartily agreed with her assessment of this being a gross waste of time and taxpayers' money.

"Megan, I don't believe these gentlemen are asking you to exchange your license to practice law for a secret decoder key. They are merely asking you to alter your vacation plans slightly. Instead of driving to Cape Cod—where I hear it has been raining for the past two weeks anyway—they want to send you to the Bahamas to soak up the sunshine. Is that so terrible?"

Megan tapped a long, perfectly manicured fingernail on the wooden arm of her chair. "It is if I don't know the reason why. Besides, the house on the Cape has already been booked and paid for. *And* as you well know, we A.D.A.'s are not exactly slotted into the top percentile of the wage bracket."

Knowing Megan Worth could have bought and sold half the property on the Cape at the mere mention of her father's name, Phil nonetheless smiled pontifically. "I have no doubt, Megan, that these gentlemen from the treasury department have come fully prepared to make fair and equitable arrangements to reimburse your out-of-pocket expenses. Moreover, I'm sure they will not only reimburse you for the Cape Cod holiday, but will willingly cover any and all expenses incurred in Freeport. Gentlemen? Have I stated that about right?"

One of the three strangers, a short man fastidiously dressed in a dark pin-striped suit, stepped forward, scowling as much over the glint of amusement in Levy's eyes, as over the cool blonde who seemed bent on making a nightmare of paperwork of what was left of his day.

"Naturally we will make all reasonable reparations, Miss Worth, in exchange for your cooperation."

Megan studied the little man. His badge identified him as a senior agent with the treasury department, but his appearance and manners reminded her of a bug exterminator. Small, piglet eyes, made smaller by wire-rimmed spectacles, peered at her along a nose that was pink and irritated by a head cold. His hand had been clammy when she had shaken it, and he had with-drawn it hastily as if the contact had offended him.

She crossed one leg over the other and picked a fleck of lint off the raspberry-colored silk cuff of her blouse. "You have not yet given me ample reason why I *should* cooperate, Agent Hornsby. You're suggesting that I can help you with a case you have been working on for nearly two years—which by your own admission, has reached a dead end—but you have not explained how I might be of assistance."

Agent Abner Hornsby smiled thinly. He signaled to one of his colleagues, an equally pretentious-looking drone, who stepped forward like an army corporal and presented Hornsby with a large manilla envelope.

"Perhaps we can begin by refreshing your memory." Opening the envelope, Hornsby withdrew several shiny black-and-white photographs. The first was an origi-nal surveillance photo of four men; the other two were enlargements of men caught by the camera's eye.

"Vincent Giancarlo," Megan murmured, frowning as she identified the central figure in the photographs. "Wasn't he in court last year on charges of tax eva-sion?"

"An excellent memory, Miss Worth. Indeed he was. Unfortunately, the charges were unsubstantiated—as usual—and he managed to avoid prosecution. A tem-porary condition, I can assure you, for *I* am deter-mined to put the man behind bars."

You and a hundred others like you, Megan thought wryly. Giancarlo was an *alleged* syndicate kingpin, his family one of three that figured prominently under the umbrella protection of Don Carlos Vannini, again *al-*

legedly one of the most powerful Mafia dons in the country.

Don Vannini was well into his eighties, and, if rumors were to be believed, he had spent the past few decades cleaning up his businesses, proving that fortunes could be made and maintained working above the law . . . or at least, very close to the line of the law.

Vincent Giancarlo was one of the last holdouts. His profits were still heavily dependent upon illegal gambling and narcotics. As well, it was suspected that he had personal control over one of the biggest money-laundering operations on the East Coast.

"You first saw these photos several months ago," Hornsby said. "Closer to a year, to be precise. Am I correct?"

Megan shot a glance at Phil Levy, who could only offer a puzzled shrug in return.

"I see a lot of photographs in the course of my job, Mr. Hornsby. If you say I saw these particular photos a year ago, I have no reason to disbelieve you."

"Then perhaps you will humor me and focus your attention on the second face from the left."

Humor him? Megan thought irritably. She caught Phil's eye again and conveyed a sense of exactly how she might like to *humor* Agent Abner Hornsby.

"All right," she said. "I'm focusing. What am I supposed to be seeing?"

The quality of the original photo was poor, the picture having been snapped at a distance through a gap in a chain-link fence. The enlargements were markedly worse, grainy and smeared, rendering the profile of the man in question nearly obscure. Making identification even more difficult, his face was half turned from the camera, leaving not much more than an impression of an angular jaw and a windswept mane of rather long, dark hair.

"I'm sorry, but I just don't—" She felt an icy prickle skitter across the nape of her neck.

"Yes, Miss Worth?" Agent Hornsby pressed forward eagerly. He had eaten garlic for lunch, and the sharp scent of his breath startled away the memory.

Megan shook her head. The chill had passed, leaving nothing in its wake but an annoyed curiosity.

"Would it help if I repeated a direct quote, noted by one of our agents at the time of your initial viewing of these photographs?"

"I don't see how it would, but I have a feeling you're going to tell me anyway, so go ahead."

"Your exact words, Miss Worth, were, 'Who is this man? He looks awfully familiar.'"

"Well?" she prompted irritably. "Who is he?"

"At the time, we didn't know. The pictures were taken in Miami and he had only arrived there a day or two before our surveillance team took an interest. Having no reason to think he was important, the agents on the team concentrated their efforts, as usual, on Giancarlo and left Mr. Michael Vallaincourt to go on his merry way."

"Michael Vallaincourt?" The name was unfamiliar and Megan said as much. "So who is he?"

"He owns a very large, very exclusive resort and casino in the Bahamas. It's called the Privateer's Paradise. At first, we had no reason to believe he had any connection with either Vincent Giancarlo or Don Carlos Vannini, so his name and picture were filed after a cursory report."

"I take it something happened to change your mind?"

"He showed up in Miami again, four times in three weeks."

"A hanging offence, I'm sure," she mused dryly.

"Then two weeks ago, he arrived in Miami very late at night and remained sequestered with Vince Giancarlo for several days."

"I still don't see what any of this has to do with me."

Hornsby held up his finger and paused for effect before he continued. "It was deemed noteworthy enough to investigate further. Imagine our surprise, when we discovered that our mysterious Mr. Vallaincourt . . . had no past. The name—apparently French—is phony. Tracing it led to a dead end. And you can see how effective we have been in capturing him on film. The security equipment in his casino affects camera film, and since he lives in the hotel, no one has been successful in trailing his movements off the grounds. In short, he is a man with no name, no face, and no past, Miss Worth. Rather a dangerous combination of unknowns, especially when matched with Giancarlo's penchant for secrecy."

Megan looked at Hornsby. He seemed to be waiting for her to offer an opinion, so she shrugged and said, "Couldn't he and Giancarlo just be friends?"

"Men like Vincent Giancarlo do not have friends. They have rivals and they have enemies."

"Then I would have to say your Mr. Vallaincourt is a bona fide challenge. The kind that should keep you happily polishing your spyglasses for months to come."

"That is just the point, Miss Worth," he countered, bristling at the sarcasm. "We have already wasted too many man-hours on Vincent Giancarlo, with very few results. If he is thinking of moving some of his business interests off the mainland, it is imperative we confirm our suspicions as soon as possible. If, as we suspect, the casino has already been tested as a venue for laundering syndicate money, then it becomes doubly important for us to know exactly what the connection is between Vincent Giancarlo and Michael Vallaincourt. The chance, however remote, you might be able to help us identify Vallaincourt, is well worth the effort of convincing you to take a paid vacation."

"But if I said he looked familiar, it could only have been—" she waved a hand, searching for some plausible explanation "—because he *does* look familiar. I mean, he looks like any one of a thousand men who pass by on the streets every day. I could have seen him anywhere."

Agent Hornsby tried to contain his impatience, but there was an increasingly shrill edge to his voice as he asked her to study the pictures again.

"I don't have to study them again, Mr. Hornsby," she said frostily. "I don't recognize the face and I don't recognize the name. I appreciate your concerns, but from what you've told me, it seems clear you would be much better off sending a trained agent."

"We could, of course. Indeed, we will have another agent in place when you arrive. But a permanent operative takes weeks, *months* to put in position."

Hornsby glared at Megan, to no visible effect. As calm and level as her gaze was now, he was almost positive he had seen a flicker of something in the vivid green depths when he had first directed her attention to the picture of Michael Vallaincourt. There was no reason to believe she was deliberately concealing information from him. After all, she was Levy's protégé and was being groomed to step into his shoes. Moreover, she came from a wealthy and influential family. Her father occupied a bench in the Supreme Court, her older brothers were both in politics. Megan herself had been weaned on the judicial system, and nowhere in her past was there any hint of a connection with anyone who had anything other than Ivy League blue blood. The Ice Queen was the genuine article, and yet . . .

"It was not my intention to make more of the situation than it perhaps is, Miss Worth, or to frighten you into thinking there is any more to it than a simple request to help identify a face. If your personal safety concerns you—"

"My concern, sir, is that I would be wasting my time as well as yours," she broke in testily.

"We are willing to risk that. The expense has already been allocated and approved. You may look upon it as a wild-goose chase, but in my experience, some of the wildest long shots have provided the missing key to a puzzle. If there is the slightest chance you can help us, then we are obliged to convince you to do so."

Megan's eyes flashed a warning that caused Philip Levy's stomach muscles to spasm as she turned to him.

"Phil, this is ridiculous. Can't you do something?"

"Frankly, no one thinks this is a bigger waste of time than I do," Phil replied wearily. "But the harsh reality is, the request has been rubber-stamped by the Attor-

ney General's office. We don't have any hard evidence
to suggest that Giancarlo is thinking of expanding his
operations. On the other hand, we do know he laun-
ders a lot of syndicate money through his businesses in
Miami. If he has shifted some of that to the Bahamas...?" Phil left the sentence open to speculation for
a moment, then shut it down with a wry twist of his
mouth. "Personally, I think it's all horse hockey. I'm not
saying I don't think that crafty bastard isn't up to
something, but take his business out of Miami? Nah.
He knows Vannini isn't long for this world and he isn't
going to give up something it took him all these years
to establish, just because some old man wants to die
with a clear conscience. But hey, that's something to
worry about in the future. For now, all these pencil-
pushers want is a positive I.D. on Vallaincourt. At best,
you'll see him up close and report back that he reminds
you of Mickey Mouse's Uncle Fred. At worst, you and
your cousin will have a two-week, all-expenses-paid
vacation at a five-star resort in the Grand Bahamas.
Please—" he pressed his hands together in supplica-
tion "—humor an old man. I retire in ten months. Take
the vacation. Take the secret decoder key and learn how
to tap out four-letter words in Morse code. It won't kill
you and it just may keep my ulcers from burning a hole
through to the seat of my pants. Speaking of which,
where'd I put my Maalox, dammit?"

While Phil rummaged fretfully through a cluttered
bottom drawer of his desk, Megan glared out the window, noting that the earlier threat of gray skies and

distant thunder had amplified into driving winds and heavy rainfall.

She wasn't being given much choice. She uncrossed her legs and stood, prolonging the tense silence by smoothing a nonexistent wrinkle from her skirt.

"Supposing . . . just *supposing* I agree to this nonsense, and I do recognize Michael Vallaincourt, what then?"

"Then?" Hornsby rushed forward, pathetically eager. "Then you simply pass the information on to one of our agents and carry on with your vacation as if nothing had ever happened to interrupt it."

Nothing, Megan thought, except perhaps having identified some social deviant she had once had occasion to prosecute.

"Don't worry, Miss Worth," Hornsby added in his most patronizing tone. "You will be perfectly safe. The Privateer is one of the most exclusive and popular resorts on the islands. Our Mr. Vallaincourt is hardly the type to fit his paying guests with cement shoes . . . regardless of the provocation."

Megan concentrated on not reaching over and shaking him until his teeth rattled. "About this decoder key . . . ?"

"Ah. Yes, well. The agent we send down to act as your conduit will be under very specific orders not to break cover or violate your privacy unless you yourself initiate contact. Since we are not sure what we are dealing with here, I would ask that you not jeopardize his cover unless you have something definitive to report."

"And just how do I initiate contact?" Megan asked testily. "By hanging a sheet out the bedroom window?"

Agent Hornsby flushed and Phil Levy grinned through a chalky, white antacid moustache.

"Naturally, we cannot trust the telephone lines, so if you do have something to relay, we would ask that you wear this bracelet—" He beckoned to his colleague again who produced a plain gold circlet from his breast pocket. "Our agent will of course know you, so, when you do need to initiate contact, put the bracelet on. When he sees you wearing it, he will contact you and that will be the end of it."

The end of it, she thought. Why didn't she believe him?

"You have the tickets, I presume?"

The third agent quickly stepped forward and handed her a well-stuffed envelope. "Airline tickets and confirmed reservations at the Privateer's Paradise," he said. "One for you—we took the added precaution of registering you under your ex-husband's name, I hope you don't mind—and one for Miss . . . ah, Stevenson, I believe it is?"

Megan drew a deep breath and groaned inwardly. What the devil was Shari going to make of all this?

Shari Stevenson was not only her cousin, but her closest friend. She had been badgering Megan to take a vacation for months, and had been on the phone each and every night for the past three weeks begging, pleading, threatening Megan not to come up with any of the dozens of excuses she had used in the past to foil holiday plans.

While she wasn't exactly canceling, Megan would still have to do some heavy-duty scheming to come up with a diplomatic way to break the news of their changed destination. After all, there were neither highways nor train tracks crossing over to the Bahamas, and, since Shari had a morbid fear of flying, getting her on a plane made the prospect of dealing with cement shoes pale by comparison.

1

MEGAN WATCHED the glittering silver ball chase around the upper rim of the roulette wheel and wondered how she could feel ridiculous and excited at the same time. It was ridiculous to think the ball would drop into the slot corresponding to the numbered square she had chosen on the green baize tabletop, yet it was exciting to think that somehow, magically, incredibly, it would.

Logic told her she was squandering a five-dollar chip. The image of a red-nosed grunion in a pin-striped suit made her smile vengefully and place the chip on number seven, black.

Almost instantly, a large freckled hand shot out in her wake and divided a small stack of red chips among the squares surrounding the black seven.

Megan stared at the barricade of red chips, then followed the freckled hand as it was retracted by its owner, an equally large and freckled Texan.

"Sometimes it works, gal, sometimes it don't," he said with a grin.

"It certainly doesn't seem to be working too well tonight," she mused aloud, feeling somewhat guilty over her poor choice of numbers thus far. Five times she had laid her five-dollar chip on a selected square, and five times the Texan had built his small Alamo of hundred-dollar chips around it. As a betting system, Megan was sure he could have dreamed up something better, although he claimed to have had surprising success with it in the past.

"It's all in the aura," he had explained sagely, pronouncing the word *ay-roo*. "And yours looks as bright and shiny as a double-eagle gold piece. Means somethin' good's gonna happen. Somethin' unexpected. Somethin'—" he had leaned forward with a conspiratorial wink "—lucky. Not that I'm superstitious ner nothin'," he added and straightened again, "but luck has a funny way o' rubbin' off on the next fella in line, and by jeez, that might as well be me as anyone else."

Megan liked the Texan. His enthusiasm was as contagious as the deep-bellied chuckle he used to emphasize his comments to the other players on the table. He had a crinkly, infectious smile, and bright blue eyes that slewed after every shapely pair of legs that strolled by. He could have been the image of a kindly old grandfather except for the smother of gold he wore on his fingers, wrists and throat. Even more jarring was the presence of the smilingly vacuous young woman he wore attached to his arm.

He had introduced himself as Dallas, though whether the name credited his ancestry or his preference of cities was never made clear. But he was bold and noisy and exuberant—good company for Megan, who could think of nothing worse than sitting alone on a bar stool and gambling away small colored chips on the whim of a silver ball.

Well, no. There was one thing worse, Meg conceded; she experienced a pang of guilt as she thought of poor Shari back in their bungalow, shaken and green about the gills, dividing her time between sitting on the toilet and bending over it. Her white-lipped terror of flying, combined with the effects of too much complimentary rum to dull the fear, had taken its toll, keeping Shari confined to their room for the past twenty-four hours.

Stoically she had insisted that Megan enjoy the sun and surf, commanding her to dine on fresh conch chowder and sip purple drinks out of split coconut shells. She had not even had the strength to lift a curious eyebrow when Meg had casually mentioned that she might take in the sights of the casino tonight. Games of chance—indeed, games of any kind—had never played much of a role in Megan's life, and, had Shari been in full possession of her senses, as well as her uncanny instinct for sniffing out trouble, she might have pounced all over Meg's interest in the casino.

Megan was just as happy she hadn't. She had thought it best not to tell Shari anything about Agent Hornsby or his harebrained schemes. Knowing Shari as well as she did, she reckoned her cousin would have undoubtedly purchased them both trench coats and fedoras and spent the entire two weeks slinking in and out of dark corners in search of intrigue.

Megan preferred to do what she had to do, get it over with and get on with her vacation. And in truth, under the sunshine and the dazzling effects of the crystalline blue sea, she had almost managed to put the entire affair out of her mind. The sand on the beach was as pink as a child's blush, the water a mélange of the most startling shades of blue, from brightest turquoise to darkest, deepest sapphire. There was far too much

peace here, and far too much beauty to waste time on
the overactive imaginings of some underpaid government lackey. That was why, with the gentle warmth of
a day in the sun fresh on her cheeks, Megan found herself sitting on an oak stool at a roulette table, hoping
against hope she would see the elusive Michael Vallaincourt before the hungry grumblings of her stomach drove her into the crowded dining room.

The Privateer's Paradise deserved its name. It was
one of the most luxurious resorts in the Bahamas,
boasting two hundred and fifty deluxe suites as well as
a five-star restaurant and a casino. Curved in a sprawling semicircle behind the main building were clusters
of private bungalows, each with its own cobblestone
terrace fronting the beach. Snorkeling, skin diving,
sailing, and sight-seeing excursions were available on
site. Or a guest could stretch out on one of the scores
of padded lounge chairs and concentrate on toasting
themselves to a golden brown.

The casino was noisy, crowded and fast-paced. The
same tourists who lazily wandered the beaches by day
in torn cutoffs and rubber thongs descended the crimson-carpeted stairs of the casino after dark like schools
of piranha scenting blood. The rich and not-so-rich
tested their luck side by side at tables of roulette, faro,
blackjack and craps. Women dressed in sequined designer gowns sat beside other women in K-Mart sun-
dresses, neither seeming to think either was out of
place.

The cavernous interior had been lavishly decorated
like a pirate's den, garish and brazen with its crimson
wall coverings and gold leaf moldings. Slot machines

in every size and shape, built to swallow coins in every denomination, were recessed into curtained alcoves that lined every foot of available wall space. Overhead, massive fans aided the air conditioning in sucking away the heat and smoke, drawing it upward into the vaulted reaches of the beamed ceiling.

The air reeked of money won and lost. Drinks were downed like water, and instantly refilled by girls dressed in silky harem costumes. There were no windows, no clocks, no means of determining if it was day or night. Megan's wristwatch had stopped shortly after she had walked through the huge arched doorway and, recalling Hornsby's comments about the security system, she wondered if there was also some kind of magnetic field built into the walls to discourage anyone from worrying over the passing of time.

Megan could only hazard a guess at the hour. She had entered the casino while the early dinner crowds were just beginning to converge in the lobby, and her best estimate, aided by the encroaching stiffness in her rump, told her she had been seated at the roulette table for a couple of hours.

So far there had been no sight of anyone even remotely resembling the blurred profile in the photo. Conversely, after two hours of surreptitiously studying the face of every man who walked by, she was ready to swear they all bore some resemblance to the grainy features in the photo Hornsby had shown her.

"Place your bets, *mesdames et messieurs*. Place your bets."

Megan glanced at the croupier, a tall dour man, Spanish in appearance, wearing a face that would have cracked before betraying any emotion.

She checked her meager pile of chips. Having set a limit of one hundred dollars to squander on testing Agent Hornsby's blood pressure, she realized half was already gone. Moreover, she did not want to disillusion Dallas's theory of *ay-roos* by prolonging his agony, and so, with a nonchalant sweep of her wrist, she placed her last ten chips together on the baize tabletop.

And why not, she thought. The noise from her stomach was getting more audible. Vallaincourt was nowhere in sight. Maybe tomorrow...

A sudden ground swell of cheers—voices and laughter raised in rowdy celebration of a win nearby—caught Megan's attention. Something else, a chill or a prickle of apprehension, made her turn her head slowly around and stare at the man who had just entered the main doors of the casino.

Eyes wide, she was aware of an achingly loud pulse beat hammering to life in her ears. It was him, the man in the blurred photograph. Despite the graininess and the poor quality of the picture, there could be no mistaking the lean, square-jawed profile. Even more conclusive was that his face was indeed familiar. Breathtakingly, heartbreakingly familiar. But when she had known him, his name had been Michael Antonacci, not Vallaincourt, and she had been as hopelessly, desperately in love with him as any self-respecting schoolgirl suffering her first unrequited crush.

It had been fifteen years since she had last seen Michael Antonacci, yet it might as well have been yesterday. Along with the hammering in her ears, she could feel the schoolgirl flush rising in her cheeks, and the giddiness starting to churn in her belly. Her mouth went dry and her skin rippled with goose bumps; to make the slightest movement suddenly seemed a monumental task and was accomplished only with a massive concentration of will.

Michael·Antonacci.

He had traded the leather jacket and faded denim jeans for a tailored silk tuxedo, but it was the same hard, lean body filling it. His thick, black mane of hair was as long and wavy as it had been in his youth; the ends curled over his collar with the same roguish carelessness that caused hearts to melt and made fingers yearn to rake through its lushness. And those eyes ... luminous blue-gray, emphasized by lashes that were indecently long, they observed, assessed and reacted to their surroundings with an air of casual indifference that had not changed or diminished in fifteen years. Handsome when he was a teenager, Michael Antonacci was sensually stunning in what must be his thirty-fourth year.

Self-consciously Megan lifted a hand and smoothed back the gleaming honey-gold of her hair. It was brushed, as always, into a sleek and elegant chignon; a style that suited her oval face and long, graceful neck. Her fingers brushed her cheek, the surface of which was reacting to a mixture of too much sun and too many memories. She still fit into the same size six she had worn in high school, and despite twenty-eight-hour days at the courthouse and a diet of hastily grabbed sandwiches and gallons of black coffee, the mirror continued to reflect a smooth, flawless complexion and features not unaccustomed to earning second and third takes from passing strangers.

Flushing even hotter, she studiously lowered her gaze and stared at the dancing silver bead as it raced around the upper rim of the roulette wheel.

Michael Antonacci in a casino in the Bahamas. How perfect. It was as perfect as the bronzed tan and the expensively cut tuxedo.

"*Dix-huit noir, dix-huit noir,*" the croupier's voice droned. "Eighteen black. The lady is a winner."

"Well goddamn, girl! That's you!" Dallas roared, nudging Megan's arm with enough enthusiasm to almost break it.

Startled, Megan watched the croupier push a small paddleful of chips her way, adding them to the ten already sitting on number eighteen, black. She was vaguely aware of smiling at Dallas and responding to whatever the devil it was he was saying. When she looked up, there was no one standing on the crimson-carpeted stairs, no sign of the broad-shouldered man moving through the room, no telltale flocks of women swooning in the wake of the rugged, chiseled profile.

She blinked, then blinked again, wondering if she had simply conjured him up in her mind. She released the breath she had been holding and felt the tiny bubble of excitement burst within her. For all she knew, it hadn't been Michael Antonacci at all, only a shockingly handsome look-alike. And even if it had been Michael, what was she supposed to do about it?

Dear God, what *was* she supposed to do? Hornsby had sent her down here, at government expense, in the hopes she could identify a face in a picture. A word from her would send their bloodhounds sniffing down the right path.

Michael. After all these years. He had been the first, the only real rebel she had ever known. He was the son of an Italian immigrant, born and raised in a tenement on the Lower East Side. Sheer chance—or mischance her father would later rage—had brought him to the attention of the local parish priest, a man who believed Michael's scholastic abilities far exceeded any opportunities available to him to claw his way out of poverty. The priest had taken it upon himself to see that Michael was accepted in a school outside the dockside community, the school that Megan attended.

At first, the sight of him roaring into the parking lot on his Harley Davidson was the source of contemptuous snickers and cold snubs. He was the kiss of death for girls who lived behind ivy-covered walls and whose mothers insisted they wear hats and natty white gloves to church on Sundays. And yet there was something irresistible about him. Something thrilling and sensuous. The same kind of something that tempts a person to walk close to a caged tiger.

Megan had had about as much in common with Michael Antonacci as oil with water, yet they had noticed each other from the outset, stealing sly glances and circling warily for weeks before he had boldly approached her for a date.

One date.

That was all they had had, and more than she had needed to fall hopelessly, helplessly in love.

Everything in her life, from being the result of a planned conception to graduating with honors from Harvard Law School, had been arranged, expected and attained without a hitch or a murmur of protest. Even her marriage had been based more on a political and social alliance of families than on any true feelings.

Dating Michael had been the only blip in the otherwise smooth progression of events. One date. One evening of feeling her insides turned to butter, her knees to jelly, her blood to fire. One evening—after so many spent merely dreaming about the impossible—and then . . . he had just disappeared. He had quit school without a word and dropped out of sight. She'd never discovered what had become of him.

"*Trente-trois, rouge. Trente-trois, rouge.* Thirty-three red . . . the lady wins again."

The croupier was skimming his wooden paddle forward, this time adding four impressive columns of colored chips to those Megan had absently shifted onto the winning square.

"Well, if that don't beat all," Dallas muttered good-naturedly, frowning as his own chips were being raked away. "Lucy darlin', maybe y'all should try the little lady's system. Ogle a handsome feller and let your pinkies choose their own numbers."

He gave the brunette a playful tweak on the arm and launched a broad wink in Megan's direction. She opened her mouth to explain her distraction, but a shadow over Dallas's shoulder stopped the words cold in her throat.

The tiger had come closer . . . close enough that she could have stretched out a hand and touched him.

Michael Antonacci was standing not four feet away. He had joined the company of two other men, one of whom he apparently knew well enough to greet with a slight nod. The other earned the full benefit of the Antonacci charm.

It *was* Michael, there was no mistake. This close, Megan could clearly see he hadn't changed a bit. There were a few more lines at the corners of his eyes, perhaps, and the glint of a few silver threads running through the jet-black waves at his temples. But if anything, the years had honed and hardened the lanky promise of youth; his shoulders were broader, bulkier with muscle, his waist as trim and tapered as an athlete's. His hands had always been strong and powerful, and, as Megan watched the exchange of pleasantries, she saw the gleam of a gold signet ring. The ring had belonged to his father and had been on Michael's hand since his fingers had grown thick enough to wear it.

Something else, something about the ring teased Megan's memory, but it was swept away on a flood of stronger remembrances as the sound of Michael's soft baritone drifted toward her.

"Now that you have had a chance to look us over," he was saying, "what do you think?"

The short, stubby stranger glanced admiringly around at the glamour and glitter of the casino. "I am impressed, Mr. Vallaincourt. I can see that you have put a lot of yourself into the Privateer."

"All I did was dot a few *i*'s and cross a few *t*'s. The casino practically runs itself."

"Profitably, too, I imagine."

Michael smiled. "None of us is suffering."

"Mr. Romani—" the man turned slightly to acknowledge the presence of the third member of their group, a barrel-chested man who stood a full head and shoulders taller than him, and was at least a foot broader across the shoulders "—has been very gracious in showing me around."

"Gino is known for his graciousness, if not his sense of humor. I hope he hasn't bored you with too many dry details."

"I am always fascinated by the mechanics of a well-oiled machine, Mr. Vallaincourt, and yours appears to be extremely well-oiled indeed. You should have no difficulty whatsoever introducing our new... *technology* to your existing systems."

"I'm pleased you think so, Mr. Samosa. I'll sleep much better tonight knowing you approve."

Samosa permitted a perfunctory smile. "In that case, I shall make the necessary calls and get back to you as soon as possible with the final details of the delivery. You understand the terms of the sale?"

The faintest shiver of contempt pulled at the corner of Michael's mouth. "I understand the principle of free enterprise, Samosa, but the latest figures you've shown me have been somewhat *freer* than we anticipated. I will have to make a few calls of my own before guaranteeing anything."

The man stiffened. "If you are referring to my commission, Vallaincourt, it was made perfectly clear from the outset. If you have a problem with it, I suggest you take a few hours to think it over, make your calls, then get back to me before my flight leaves in the morning. Naturally, after an investment of so much time and effort, it would be a shame to have to find another buyer, but I assure you, it can be done."

He gave a curt bow and turned away. A fourth man who had been hovering a few feet away, fell instantly into step behind the retreating Samosa, splitting a caustic look between Michael and Gino Romani before walking away.

"Well, well, well," Gino breathed. "Cocky little bastard, isn't he? Think he means it?"

"I think he's bluffing, and not very well. Somewhere between here and Venezuela he's padded his fee, and I think he'll be the one spending a few warm hours debating the state of his health."

Michael reached into an inside pocket of his tuxedo jacket and extracted a long, thin cigarillo. "I'll just be glad when this whole business is over. I don't like Samosa and I don't like his Colombian friends. Most especially, I don't like being forced to play a hand when the cards are being marked right under our eyes."

"It's all part of the game, Mikey," Gino said, holding out a lighter. "Don't let it get to you now, not when we're this close."

Megan stared at Gino's hand as he returned the gold lighter to his inside pocket. The unbuttoned edges of his jacket were displaced a second time and she caught a confirming sight of what she had only glimpsed a moment ago.

Gino was wearing a gun.

The holster was small and tucked discreetly into the hollow of his armpit, but it was there nonetheless, housing a compact, snub-nosed automatic. The sight of it had sent all of Megan's instincts bristling—all of those not already standing on end over the conversation she'd overheard. It was hardly any wonder she had few faculties left to react to the delayed realization that Samosa had addressed Michael Antonacci as Michael Vallaincourt, or that the pale blue-gray eyes, accustomed to scanning the crowds, began to slowly turn in her direction.

"*Cinquante-deux, rouge. Cinquante-deux, rouge.* Fifty-two red," the croupier shouted. "And again the lady wins!"

"How 'bout that, missy! Dang me if y'all ain't done it again!" The Texan's beetling white eyebrows flew upward and he thumped Megan's shoulder hard enough to send her hand jumping forward against her cocktail glass. The glass tipped, spilling the contents down the hem of her silk sundress in its tumble to the floor.

"Aw, shoot, darlin', I'm sorry. Look what I've gone and done. Here, let me help."

"No! No, please." Megan stopped Dallas's hand before he could flourish the flag-size handkerchief he had been using all evening to blow his nose. "It was only water from the melted ice. Anyway, it was my own fault for putting the glass so close to the edge of the table and not paying attention to what I was doing."

"Well, for someone who ain't payin' attention, gal, y'all sure are pickin' your numbers right. Three wins in a row, blast it, and me settin' here with my thumb up my ass just a-watchin'."

Megan smiled faintly and finished blotting the few splashes of water off her dress. Most of it had spilled onto the carpet. The real damage was measured in the number of curious eyes fixed in her direction—one pair in particular.

Worse, when she bent down to retrieve the glass, a second hand was there ahead of hers, the gold of the heavy signet ring causing the sting of embarrassment to remain hot in her cheeks.

For the longest moment, she just stared at the ring hoping she could compose herself enough to look up into his face. When she did, it was by cowardly degrees—sleeve, shoulder, neck, jaw . . .

There had always been something dark and dangerous about Michael Antonacci's face: the smile that was never quite a smile; the jaw that was too square to be decent; the teeth too straight and white to be anywhere but in a toothpaste commercial. Each feature was enough to make a woman grow damp, but when commanded by the blatantly seductive teal blue of his eyes . . .

This is ridiculous, Megan chided herself. You are a grown woman now, not a love-struck teenager. You have been married and divorced, you have encountered your fair share of handsome, successful men over the years without falling to pieces over a smile.

"I hope you will allow me to order you a fresh drink," Michael was saying. "It would be a shame to break your lucky streak over a few sprinkles of water, Miss—?"

"Mrs.," she blurted, retreating behind her married name. "Mrs. Thomas. And thank you but no, I was finished playing for the night."

"It will be the first time in the casino's history that good luck has driven someone away from the tables." The luminous eyes, under their devastating sweep of black lashes, rose from the darkened spatter on her skirt, not in any apparent hurry to outrun the dull red heat that had crept up her throat and into her cheeks. Megan was left with the distinct impression he had inspected every inch of naked flesh beneath the amber-colored sundress, probing for anything that might be remotely interesting to a man of his selective tastes.

"Are you a guest in the hotel?" he inquired politely, the slightest blur of a frown drawing the slash of his eyebrows together.

"Yes. Yes, I am." Don't remember me now, Megan pleaded. She averted her head quickly, covering her sudden awkwardness by gathering up the astonishingly large pile of playing chips she had won.

"Then at least allow me to cover any valet expenses for having your dress cleaned."

"Allow you? But it was an accident. My own clumsy fault, to be precise. And you were a dozen feet away at the time—" She stopped again, halted by the crooked smile that acknowledged her admission that she'd been aware of his presence earlier.

That did the trick. The flutter in her belly ground to a standstill, the tremor in her hands disappeared, leaving them cool and steady. She finished scooping her winnings into the small plastic treasure chest provided for the purpose, and slung the strap of her purse over her shoulder.

"Thank you for the offer, but it really isn't necessary. It was only water."

"And it is only my reputation as host that you are putting at stake here," he warned softly. "Michael Vallaincourt," he added, holding out his hand by way of an introduction. "I own the Privateer's Paradise."

"Yes, I know," she blurted. "I . . ."

His gaze, briefly distracted by an outburst of laughter from another table, sliced back to hers and for a moment, seemed to climb right inside her skin.

"Yes?"

"Nothing," she said quickly. "I . . . it was nothing. If you will excuse me now, I have had a very long day."

He tipped his head courteously and stepped to one side to let her pass. "I hope you will enjoy the rest of your stay with us, Mrs. Thomas. If there is anything you need, or anything I can do for you, please feel free to come and see me."

Conscious of other eyes on her—including Dallas's, twinkling with retrained humor—Megan murmured her thanks and made a hurried exit from the casino. Her hand, indeed, her whole arm was still tingling from the effects of the handshake; she was barely aware of walking though the marble lobby and finding the corridor that led outside to the private bungalows. Behind and above her was the enormous terraced restaurant, its patio bathed russet in the orange-red flare of the sunset. The muted throb of a steel band followed her along the crushed stone walkway that circled the swimming pool, and, had she been in the frame of mind to turn and look behind her, she might have noticed the tall, tuxedo-clad figure of the man who had followed her as far as the edge of the terrace, and who stood there now, staring thoughtfully after her.

2

"SO WHAT'S the big mystery?" Shari demanded crossly, holding her head in both hands as if it would have spun away otherwise. "A lot of people change their names when they move around."

"A lot of people move around, they don't necessarily change their names unless they have a damned good reason for doing so."

"Okay, okay, so shoot the guy. He's obviously guilty of every heinous crime known to man."

"His family was ... connected ... if you know what I mean," Megan said, lowering her voice for emphasis.

"So are half the Italians in New York State. Why should that surprise you?"

"There was a rumor at school that his brother was in jail for murder. For all I know, Michael could have become involved in similar activities. He did vanish two months before he was supposed to graduate."

"Maybe he just hated school. Maybe he was flunking out anyway."

"No. He was actually quite smart," Megan recalled with a frown. "The effortless kind of smart, you know? He never had to work at it like the rest of us, never used the time in study hall to study. I don't think he ever cracked the spine of a textbook."

"Then he must be guilty," Shari replied dryly. "Shoot the bastard, by all means."

Megan stared down at the paper cocktail umbrella she was twirling between her fingers. Her eyes strayed to the puckered water spots on her dress, replaying for the hundredth time the events in the casino. She had been visibly shaken by the encounter—enough for Shari to notice through her nausea and demand an explanation. Telling her cousin she had seen a ghost from the past seemed the closest thing to the truth, and it would have to do until she decided what her next move should be.

By rights, she should find the bracelet Hornsby had given her and wear it prominently until some nameless shadow sought her out. She should advise the treasury agent of Michael's real name and leave the unraveling of the mystery to those better equipped to handle unpleasant and unwanted surprises. And there was every possibility it *would* be unpleasant. Michael Antonacci was smart. He had the nerve and the eye for danger. Just the fact he had become the owner of one of the richest resorts on the islands opened his past to speculation.

As if reading her thoughts, Shari sighed and ran a hand through the tightly curled tangle of her short red hair. "Oh, come on. Lighten up. He isn't an ax murderer or he wouldn't own a famous resort in the Bahamas. On the other hand, if he does own it, he must be a very good, very clever criminal."

"You're a big help."

"You're the one taking your job too seriously. You've been around thieves and crooks so long you wouldn't recognize an honest entrepreneur if you tripped over one. So maybe this Michael had a questionable youth, but hey—who didn't? Every school had its resident hood—jeans and leather jacket, studs inside their pants as well as out. Guys who thought *The Godfather* was a training film. It doesn't mean they all went into a life of crime and conspiracy. Most of them are probably fat and balding and playing baseball with their twelve kids every Sunday afternoon, which is why I make a point of never attending any school reunions. I hate having my illusions shattered. Damn—" she adjusted her position on the mountain of pillows she had commandeered and refolded the damp facecloth she was holding across her forehead. "I feel awful. Is there any tea left in the pot?"

"It will be ice-cold by now," Megan guessed, uncurling her legs from the seat of the chair and standing. "Do you want me to call room service and order more?"

Shari opened her mouth to answer, but had a funny look wash over her face instead. She swallowed what she had been about to say along with a mouthful of dry, sour air. Her normally smooth complexion was waxen, her mop of curly hair was plastered flat to her scalp. Her eyes, usually a vibrant, mischievous blue were red-rimmed and puffed half-closed.

"I don't believe this," she groaned. "Two weeks in the Bahamas. Two glorious weeks of sun and sand and doing nothing more strenuous than slapping on another coat of suntan oil . . . and where am I? What am I doing? Clinging to life and hanging over the basin of a five-star bidet."

"It's all in your mind."

"It certainly isn't in my stomach, anymore," she agreed with a moan.

"I warned you about dosing yourself with island rum to relieve your stress. I'd be willing to bet most of what you are feeling stems from that, not the flight."

Shari stuck out her tongue and Megan laughed. "Believe it or not, you do look a lot better than you did this morning. A good night's sleep and you'll be your usual irritating self in the morning."

Shari groaned and rolled onto her side, hiccuping softly. "I hate flying. You know I hate flying. Couldn't you have come up with some other way of torturing me—pins under my fingernails, fiberglass in my underwear?"

"You wanted me to pass up a free trip?"

"A suspiciously free trip, Meggy my dear, and don't think, for one moment, I won't be able to wriggle a better explanation out of you than 'someone in the office had the tickets and couldn't use them.' You've only been spared the electrodes this long because I've been too busy devising a suitable revenge on my psychoanalyst. Mind over matter, my ass. It would serve him right if I get off the plane back in New York and die right in his lap." Another odd look flushed across her face and she wailed through a curse. "And we do have to fly back, don't we?"

"You'll survive." Megan crossed over to the dresser and wrinkled her nose in distaste as she lifted the stopper on the silver thermos of tea. "But not if you drink this. Do you want me to order a refill?"

"Don't bother. I would probably only see it again in a far more ghastly state an hour from now. Sit back down. Talk to me for a while. I took some more Dramamine a while ago and, without wanting to sound too hopeful, I do believe the carousel in my brain is starting to slow down a bit. Tell me what I missed today. The boredom in your voice will put me to sleep if nothing else."

"I had a quiet, relaxing day."

"Fine. Now say it without gritting your teeth."

"Honestly, I had a very nice, relaxing day. I breakfasted early on our own charmingly secluded patio—" Megan swept her hand toward the sliding doors that were a feature in both their bedrooms and the connecting sitting room "—afterward, I laid on the beach and started reading a rather intriguing romance novel."

One bleary eye levered open warily. "Romance novel? You read romance novels?"

"I'm not completely numb from the neck down, you know. And I do read more than political briefs and law books. Besides, I thought it was high time I found out exactly how it was you earn your livelihood."

Shari blushed so darkly, her bright red hair looked like a flame atop her head.

"How did you find out?" she squeaked.

"Deductive reasoning."

"Melvin Pimble." Shari sighed with chagrin. "I knew I shouldn't have asked you for the name of a good business lawyer. Whatever happened to attorney-client privilege?"

"Mel had no idea your career was supposed to be a secret. He merely thanked me for referring a famous novelist to him. Oh, and he said to tell you that his wife loves your books—especially the one about the...wait a minute, now, I want to get this quote right . . . about the socialite assistant district attorney with the touch-me-and-die attitude toward men who ends up falling head over heels in love with some itinerant trucker. Mel wondered if you had anyone specific in mind when you modeled your heroine."

Shari swallowed hard, the blush still raging in her cheeks.

"Touch me and die?" Megan queried sardonically.

"Well . . . I needed a good, strong conflict between my characters. I needed a contrast."

"You made me out to be a frigid spinster with a Grace Kelly complex. And the hero! A leering Neanderthal with an inability to keep his fly zipped!"

Shari's eyebrows shot up to her hairline. "*That's* the romance novel you started reading?"

"*Heart of Stone* by Constance Fairbreast. Catchy pseudonym, I must admit. I never would have guessed."

Shari sank back down into the pillows. "So that's why you made me fly down here. Go ahead then, get it over with. Break my arms, or my legs, or whatever else appeals to you. But before you do, you should know that *Heart of Stone* was on the bestseller lists for ten weeks, and my agent has a movie producer interested in the rights."

"I'll sue."

"On what grounds? The heroine was beautiful and intelligent—not exactly a slanderous description. She endured an ugly marriage and an even uglier divorce—the bare facts as reported by the gossip columnists for all the world to see. If anything, I toned them down. She buried herself in her work and spent five years verbally castrating every man who tried to get close to her—so okay, you've been divorced eight years and you prefer to let the general population believe you 'enjoy your privacy.'"

"I do enjoy my privacy. And I have a very full social life, thank you very much."

"Mmm. Cozy power lunches with clients, lawyers and politicians. Very stimulating for the hormones, I'm sure."

"I'm a little past the stage of chasing after beach bums and car jockeys," Megan said.

"Absolutely. Thirty-two is certainly over the hill. And Richard wasn't a car jockey, he was a chauffeur." Shari paused and a glint came into her eyes. "With one of the nicest stick shifts I've ever driven."

"So where is he now?"

Shari sniffed. "He was a free spirit. And I resent you calling the hero of *Heart of Stone* a Neanderthal. He was big and brawny, with a chest of hair a girl could get lost in, but that's how *I* happen to like my men. Strong. Silent. Commanding."

She sighed wistfully and Megan shook her head. "You're hopeless."

Shari narrowed her eyes. "What about this old flame of yours? He seems to have sparked your hormones where others have failed."

"He wasn't a flame. Michael and I dated once, that's all."

"That's all?"

"We went to a party together, and there were so many other people around, you couldn't even call it a proper date."

"Ah-hah! So you have lingering regrets that you were never alone with him!"

"No," Meg groaned. "I do not."

"You *do*." Shari pushed herself upright and flung the damp facecloth aside like a gauntlet being flung in a challenge. "And now here he is, fifteen years later, offering you a chance to rekindle the romance."

"He offered to pay for valet service. He didn't even recognize me."

Megan walked over to the glass doors and Shari studied her cousin's profile against the faded sunset. Every golden hair was combed neatly in place. Her posture was perfect, her body sculpted to fit a man's most erotic fantasies. Success was written all over her, and yet Shari was not fooled. She had known Megan too long not to see the restlessness. She wanted everyone to think she was happy and content with her life, but she wasn't. Something was missing, and, with the keen instincts of a seasoned matchmaker, Shari thought she knew what it was.

"If he didn't recognize you," she said casually, "you could easily rectify the situation by—"

"Forget it, *Constance*," Megan warned, casting a sharp look over her shoulder. "I'm not interested in rekindling anything with Michael Antonacci... or Vallaincourt... or whatever else he calls himself. In fact, I plan to steer clear of him for the rest of the time we are here. And if you don't want to spend the next twelve months or so strapped into the seat of a twin-engine Cessna, you'll leave it alone, too."

"But aren't you the least bit curious to know what happened to him after high school, or how he came to be here, or how he ended up being so successful?"

"No," Megan said bluntly, seeing in her mind's eye the snub-nosed automatic Michael's companion had been wearing beneath his jacket. "I am not at all curious."

Shari snorted and melted back into the nest of pillows. "And I believe you, too, Megan Worth. It's what made you such a good character for my book."

3

AN HOUR LATER, it was not curiosity, but hunger that found Megan sitting at a small table on the restaurant terrace. The Dramamine Shari had taken had finally kicked in and Megan had dimmed the lights and hung the Do Not Disturb sign on the doorknob. Tiptoeing quietly out of their bungalow, she had returned through the fragrant darkness to the noise and brighter lights of the hotel.

Megan's table was by the carved balustrade, giving her a panoramic view of the pool, bungalows, beach and bay. Palm trees rustled with the warm breezes. The smell of the sun's heat was still trapped in the buildings and on the grounds, lending a special brand of perfume to the night air. Hundreds of twinkling lights were strung above the terrace, and, at each table a pagoda-shaped glass sconce glowed with a burning candle. New York was her home and she was sentimentally attached to the changing seasons, but there was something undeniably sensuous about sipping wine under the rising tropical moonlight.

Being only human, she let her thoughts regress to Michael Antonacci. And, being only human, she naturally jumped half out of her skin when she turned and saw him standing in the shadows only a few feet away, watching her.

"Forgive me, I did not mean to startle you."

"How long . . . I mean . . . where did you come from? You weren't standing there a minute ago."

"I was inside at the bar," he said. "I couldn't help but notice you when you were being shown to your table."

His gaze drifted downward and Megan's pulse rate rose proportionately. She had changed out of the water-marked silk sundress and wore another of clinging white jersey. It seemed to cling even tighter where his eyes lingered over the curve of her breasts, or perhaps it was just her own skin, constricting so tautly that the softness of the jersey seemed transformed to sandpaper.

She met his eyes again, disliking the sensation of being caught off guard twice in as many hours. Worse, as he stepped out of the shadows and into the brighter wash of the lights, she was dismayed by the shiver of molten excitement that raced down her spine.

"Megan Worth," he said quietly. "it is you, isn't it?"

There was nothing to be gained by denying it, so she smiled with what she hoped would pass for an apology and nodded. "I didn't think you recognized me in the casino, and it didn't seem the right time or place for renewing old acquaintances."

His smile widened and he eased himself comfortably into the empty seat across from her. "I didn't recognize you—not at first, anyway. Your hair—" he waved a hand and frowned "—I don't ever remember you wearing it scraped back into a bun. The name wasn't familiar, either, but I checked through the room registrations and saw 'Thomas, Ms. Megan, and Stevenson, Miss Sharon' in bungalow four. I guess it was the 'Megan' that finally twigged."

"Do you always go to so much trouble to fit a name to a face?"

"If I know the face is going to keep me up all night wondering, I do." One eyebrow arched and he glanced pointedly at the single place setting. "Are you eating alone?"

"Well, actually...yes. My cousin isn't feeling too well tonight."

"Nothing serious, I hope? We have a doctor on staff full-time. If you think he should stop by and have a look—?"

"Not unless he has any magical cures for a hangover," she said with a laugh. "Shari has a phobia about flying, and consequently suffers twice as much by trying to compensate in other than medicinal ways. She just needs a good night's sleep and she'll be her perky old self in the morning."

Perky, Megan thought. Did I actually say *perky*?

"In the meantime," she added quickly, "I've been quite content to rattle around by myself exploring. You mentioned you owned the Privateer's Paradise? I'm impressed. It is a lovely resort."

"Our goal has been achieved, then. We aim to impress. And," he sighed ruefully, "if the absolute truth be told, I only own a very small percentage of the resort. Minuscule, in fact. But saying I own it all saves a lot of unnecessary explanations. How long will you be staying with us?"

"Two weeks. I suppose it was poor planning to come south in the middle of June. We really should have saved the trip for January or February."

"Ah yes, the joys of winter and all that white stuff. I've almost forgotten what snow looks like, thank God."

"How long have you been living here?"

He pursed his lips thoughtfully. "Only two years here, but another eight or so in other tropical paradises."

"It sounds like you've suffered. Have you never been homesick for slush and sleet and the joys of black ice?"

"When I am, I take a couple of aspirins and lie down until the feeling passes. You are still living in New York?"

"I guess I'm just a city girl at heart."

"Oh, I don't know. We've had some pretty successful conversions down here. If I'm not mistaken, I hear one coming now."

A second figure emerged from the shadows, startling Megan's eyes away from Michael. It was the man from the casino, and despite his size, she had been unaware of his approach until he was almost at the table. Excusing the interruption, Gino Romani leaned over to murmur a few words in Michael's ear. Michael's teal blue eyes never left Megan's face as he listened to what Gino was saying, if he noticed any sudden tension in Megan's expression, he gave no indication.

"Fine," he said. "Just make sure the old guy countersigns the check in front of you. Gino Romani, meet an old friend of mine, Megan Worth. We grew up in the same neck of the woods, albeit on opposite sides of the tracks."

Gino smiled like a friendly bear and stuck out his hand. "Miz Worth. A pleasure."

"Mr. Romani," she murmured, responding guardedly to his handshake.

"Gino is head of security for the hotel and the casino," Michael explained. "If you have any problems at all—"

"Just give me a shout," Gino finished with a friendly wink. "Okay, Mikey, I better get back. Aren't you supposed to be on your way to George's?"

"I left ten minutes ago, if anyone asks."

"Yeah, well, time's a' wasting. Nice meeting you, Miz Worth. Enjoy your vacation."

"Thank you, I will," Megan said, her conscience experiencing both guilt and relief. There was certainly nothing sinister about the head of security carrying a gun. It was such a perfectly logical explanation, she almost laughed out loud.

"Mikey—" Gino held up a finger as if he was reminding a forgetful boy of a promise. "Be back no later than midnight, eh? And say hello to George for me."

Michael nodded and waved him away. "Good respectful help is hard to find these days. If he wasn't twice my size, I'd tell him so, too."

Megan's smile was quick to respond to his. After studying the pale halo of her silhouette for several more moments, he pushed reluctantly to his feet and, with a gesture of impatience that was still achingly familiar after all the years, raked a hand through the errant waves of his hair and sighed. "Listen, I have to be somewhere—"

"I understand perfectly—" she started to say. Whatever might have come next was held up by the unexpected touch of his hand on her shoulder.

"You said you were at loose ends for the rest of the evening—why not join me for dinner and we can reminisce over our ill-spent youth?"

"But, you said you have to be somewhere."

"I do. And it just happens to be the best damned restaurant on the island."

"Better than your own?"

"Are you kidding? The prices here are outrageous. I have three French chefs in the kitchens who do nothing all day but dream up new ways to combine heavy cream, butter and eggs into concoctions that would clog a drill sergeant's arteries overnight."

"I've already ordered something that sounds as if it would do just that," she said.

"As they say here in the islands—no problem. We can cancel it on the way out."

"Cancel, but—"

"No buts," he said and reached down to take her hand in his. The heat of contact was so sudden and fierce, she had to fight the urge to check if her skin was being singed. Fighting urges was an altogether new sensation for Megan, and she found herself standing, pulled up gently by his hand, wondering wildly if her legs would have the strength to support her.

Michael looked away to catch the attention of the waiter, and without the threat of his eyes fusing her tongue to the roof of her mouth, Megan was able to stammer out a final, feeble protestation. It faltered to dry air, however, no match for the dazzling effects of his smile.

"I have a couple of hours before the midnight revues empty and the serious gamblers show up at the casino. I like to go somewhere where I can loosen my tie and kick off my shoes without having a flurry of fingers wagged at me. Of course you will have to swear a blood oath not to reveal the location of my hideaway to any other of my high-paying guests. It's hard enough getting a parking spot at George's as it is."

She was disappointed when he released her hand, but the feeling was short-lived as Megan became instantly and acutely aware of every female eye enviously following her across the crowded room.

Had the restaurant not seemed empty and deserted only a few minutes ago?

"The early show over at the Princess must have just ended," Michael explained, steering her through the crowd of people milling about at the entrance. He cupped a hand beneath her elbow and led the way along the marble-columned lobby toward a corridor marked Private. In no time at all, they were standing in the parking lot and Megan was faced with a new dilemma: how to fold her body in half and slide elegantly into a bucket seat that was only a few inches off the ground.

"What happened to the Harley?" she wondered aloud.

Michael opened the passenger door of the candy-apple red Ferrari and grinned. "I'll bring it in tomorrow, if you like."

"You still have it?"

"It's a more modern version of the one I used to tear up the streets of the Bronx, but yes. I still like the taste of dust now and then."

Somehow the thought of Michael clinging to his image of a hell-raising rebel broke the tension Megan had been feeling and she was able, with a little assistance, to lower herself into the seat of the car with relative grace. Michael climbed in beside her, all six foot three of him sliding into the leather seat without a wink of effort, and settling into the custom-molded cockpit as if it were an extension of his own body. He slotted the key into the ignition, checked once to see if Megan's seat belt was secured, then turned the key, shattering the palm-swept silence with a tremendous burst of screaming horsepower. His hand seemed to caress the stick shift—a gesture that sent an envious wave of sparks shimmering along Megan's spine—and he swung the growling machine out of the lot and into the main street.

Streams of wandering tourists clogged both sides of the road. Some shouted and waved as the Ferrari prowled past; one or two even raised their cameras and snapped a quick picture as the gleaming red sports car drew abreast. On both occasions, Megan noticed Michael turning his face away from the bright flash, and when he turned back, there was a tight frown of annoyance pleating his forehead.

Did he just not want to be blinded by exploding flash units, Megan wondered, or did he just not like having his picture taken by strangers?

And what on earth was wrong with Hornsby's men if they could not track the whereabouts of a man who drove around Freeport in a snappy red Ferrari?

"You know, maybe this isn't such a good idea, after all," Megan began. "I feel terribly guilty just driving away without even stopping in at the bungalow to make sure Shari is okay."

"You said she was fast asleep."

"She was when I left, but I still shouldn't have driven off without a word. It isn't like me at all."

Michael glanced over. "I'm flattered to know I can still corrupt you. Don't worry, I'll have you back by midnight. She won't even know you were gone."

No one knows I've gone, Megan thought. Or where I've gone. Isn't this just the sort of thing police forces all around the world spend thousands of man-hours warning people against? Yet here she was, miles from home, in a strange country, accepting a dinner invitation from a man she hadn't seen in fifteen years—a man she had been sent specifically to Freeport to identify for the justice department.

She pictured the gold bracelet sitting in a drawer in her room, and bit the fleshy pad of her lip.

"If it bothers you that much," Michael said, glancing over, "we can call the hotel and leave a message for her at the desk. Better yet—" He lifted the small receiver of a cellular phone and pushed a few buttons before holding it to his ear. "Suzie? I think my secretary has left for the evening, but could you do me a favor? Find Gino and get him to check in on the party staying in bungalow four. The lady wasn't feeling too well this afternoon and her friend is concerned about leaving her alone. Tell Gino I have kidnapped Ms. Thomas and he's to keep an attentive eye on Miss Stevenson until we get back. That's it, thanks."

"There," he said, replacing the receiver and turning to Megan with a smile that could have melted a glacier. "Done."

"Thank you," she murmured. Feeling foolish, she sank lower in the seat. "I didn't mean to put anyone to any trouble."

"No problem."

A second burst of power from the Ferrari startled Megan's attention back to the road. They had cleared the congestion of the main thoroughfare and were gliding onto a rustically paved highway that led out of the city. The noise, the lights, the wealth of the sparkling tourist hotels was quickly left behind as the Ferrari accelerated. Conversation was impossible over the roar of the engine and in silence Megan watched the miles fly by. She tried to concentrate on the scenery, but once the city had faded from view, there was only blackness on either side of the road, and the stark glare of the car's high beams ahead. And curves. Ninety-degree turns in the snaking road that Michael carved the Ferrari around as if neither man nor machine had ever heard of gravity.

She was just beginning to unclench her teeth and adjust to the breathless exuberance of their high-speed flight, when the car braked to a crawl and slid into a gravel-covered lane. After a hundred yards or so, the lane widened into a shallow scoop of a parking lot. Butted to the edge of the water at one end, the gravel formed an apron around a rickety wooden shack that looked as if it was slowly and irretrievably settling into the bay.

Michael parked beside the only other vehicle in the lot—a rusted pickup held together by bands of looped wire—and shut down the ignition with a wistful caress. He was out of the car and opening Megan's door before the growl of the powerful engine had finished vibrating through her body. Still faintly disoriented from the speed and noise, she was only vaguely aware of Michael reaching over to unfasten her seat belt, then grasping her by both hands and helping her to her feet.

The ground shifted unsteadily beneath her and Megan leaned instinctively against the strong wall of Michael's chest for support. Wisps of hair, blown wild by the wind, had been torn out of her chignon, and it seemed a natural, familiar gesture for him to smooth the errant tendrils back from her cheek and throat. Even more natural, almost expected, he ran the backs of his fingers along the curve of her chin and tilted her face up to his.

Michael's lips brushed over hers, fleetingly at first, testing for resistance. Megan knew she should have offered some, ought to have pulled away with a laugh or a witty remark to cover her utter sense of helplessness, but a soft, breathy sigh was the best she could manage.

Michael's hands tightened, cradling her neck with a firm possessiveness. His mouth slanted more forcefully over hers, his tongue conquering another half-hearted moan, silencing it beneath a tender, languorous assault on her senses. Instead of pushing him away, Megan's hands inched higher on the broad plain of his chest, and her fingers curled under the silk lapels of his tuxedo. His body crowded hers against the side of the Ferrari and she was introduced to the muscular hardness of his thighs, belly and torso.

The kiss ended as deliberately as it had begun, with a slow retreat of taste and touch. His hands remained cupped beneath her chin and his eyes remained locked unwaveringly on hers. Megan could not think of a thing to say or do.

"I have been wanting to do that ever since I saw you in the casino," Michael murmured.

"You said you didn't . . . recognize me in the casino," she stammered.

The gleam in his eyes intensified. "Do I have to personally know every beautiful woman I see before I can fantasize about holding her in my arms and kissing her? Furthermore, now that I do . . . know you, that is . . . I seem to recall being cheated out of more than just a kiss on our one and only date. And I never like being cheated out of what's owed me."

His mouth descended again, claiming hers with a mocking vengeance that started hot and cold ribbons of sensation coiling through her body. His hands skimmed down the sides of her body and circled her waist, drawing her incredibly closer to his heat.

She remembered. . . .

They had returned from the party and were talking on the front porch. Michael had seemed hesitant, almost shy, for the first time in her recollection. When she felt as if she would burst from the waiting, he had taken her into his arms and kissed her.

She had never forgotten those few glorious, passionate moments. No one else had ever kissed her like that, before or since, and she had always wondered if the shimmering liquid thrill of her memory had been embellished and exaggerated over the years.

Now she knew.

It hadn't.

As she stood here with him now, she felt the heat living and moving within her. She was conscious of a rising, expanding urgency that grew and kept growing until her whole body became a mass of raw nerve endings. The flesh across her breasts was stretched taut with shock, with pleasure. The flesh between her thighs shivered with anticipation, filling her with a need she did not comprehend and could not control.

Gasping, she tore her lips free and for all of ten seconds, she knew a desire so powerful it frightened her. She closed her eyes, wanting to pretend it had not happened, was not happening, but his arms were still around her, and his body... his body was offering no apologies for the similar response she could feel thundering through his veins.

"I like the way you pay your debts," he said softly, his voice shaky. "Now you're making me wish your father had waited another ten minutes before bursting out at us. We could have run up quite a tab."

Megan bowed her head so that her forehead rested against the bottom of his chin. Her father had, indeed, interrupted them too soon, throwing on the porch floodlights and raging through the door like a storm cloud. He had taken one look at the position of their hands and bodies, and he had nearly wakened the whole neighborhood with his shouting.

"He and Mother had both been waiting, pacing all night long," she whispered, her embarrassment as acute now as it had been all those years ago. "He was furious to think I would have let my good name become associated with . . . with someone like you."

"Someone like me?"

"He . . . had heard some things . . ."

Michael angled her face up to his again. "People shouldn't believe everything they hear. Sometimes even what they see can lead to the wrong conclusions."

His hands dropped away and he took a step back, breaking the intimacy between their bodies. Then, as if he did not trust himself to say more, he shrugged off the seriousness of the moment with a grin and waved a hand airily in the direction of the diner. "Take this place, for example. A real dive, right? A tourist wouldn't stop here if his bus caught on fire, but just wait until you taste what George does with boiling water and a few spices."

"Do you come here often?"

"Not as often as I'd like. I hope you're hungry. George doesn't believe in small portions or delicate appetites."

"He won't be disappointed. I'm starving." Megan's pulse rate was almost back to normal and she was grateful for the few seconds of banter. She even thought she might be able to walk without stumbling over her feet.

As it turned out, Michael took Megan's hand anyway, guiding her around the wide, deep potholes gouged in the gravel parking lot years ago and evidently not worth the effort to fix. He held the screenless, squeaking door to the restaurant open, bowing her in ahead of him with a gallant flourish of his arm.

If it wasn't what he would call a dive, Megan was not sure she wanted to see what he used as a basis for comparison. The walls were rough timber, painted green in various sections and in shades that suggested the painter had let a year or two lapse between spurts of ambition. The floor was black-and-white tile, chipped and torn in places, but perfectly suited to the ambience of fly-spotted windows and sagging ceiling tiles. There were only four tables, none of them matching in size or color. Chairs were also an assortment of shapes and sizes, with extras stacked against one wall like the Leaning Tower of Pisa. Across the far wall, a counter divided the kitchen from the dining area. A door curtained with strings of wooden beads gave access to the rear, as well as to a dark, sloping hallway that led to the single, vile-looking rest room.

Despite the presence of only one car in its parking lot, the diner was full. The four tables were filled with customers—all brown and wizened and seemingly as mismatched as the contents of the building itself. Michael's appearance won a few hard looks; Megan's earned raised eyebrows and a jab or two of sharp elbows into neighboring ribs.

Almost immediately, a man with a seamed black face popped up from behind the counter, a dazzling white smile spreading ear to ear as he shouted Michael's name.

"Ooo-wee! Doan we looks fancy tonight!"

A grin tugged crookedly at Michael's lips as he escorted Megan through the beaded curtains and formally introduced the owner of the establishment as George Samson.

"Never mind no fancy Mr. Samson stuff, neither," he admonished with a friendly wink. "My friends just call me George."

"My friends just call me Meg," she countered, retrieving her hand from a surprisingly strong grip.

Viewed in the harsher light from the naked bulbs in the kitchen, George's age was still a mystery, although it seemed to verge on ancient. What little hair he had was sprinkled liberally with gray and his body was thin and bony, belted into a frayed shirt and trousers that were several sizes too big for him.

George squinted up at Michael and scratched at the sparse white stubble poking out of his chin. "I'm t'inkin' you come here slummin' again, eh mon? Doan them fancy cooks of yours know how to boil up an honest meal?"

"I wanted to impress Megan properly, show her some real island hospitality."

"Well, you comes to the right place, then," George cackled. "No problem."

Still cackling, he waved them through the kitchen— a narrow alleyway of pots, pans and huge vats of steaming water—then through another partly unhinged door, which Michael had to duck to clear. There, a wide porch clung precariously to the rear of the building, the sloping roof propped up by carved wooden posts, the eaves decorated with scalloped bits of Victorian gingerbread trim that were even older than the proprietor. A round wooden table and four chairs were set up by the railing, the latter being a wobbly, spindly thing that was the only barrier between them and the inky blue waters of the bay.

George shuffled ahead to remove two of the chairs and used the tail of his shirt to dust away the crumbs from the tabletop. The porch swayed alarmingly even under his weight, and more so when Michael and Megan walked over to take their seats. Megan caught a splash of water on her ankle and looked down, horrified to see that the porch was hanging out over the water.

"Is this safe?" she asked in a whisper, waiting until George had muttered his way inside again.

"Can you swim?"

"Of course."

"Then it's safe," Michael said blithely. "I've been coming here for two years now and I don't believe George has ever lost a customer to the sharks."

"Sharks?" Megan flinched away from the railing. "There are sharks out there?"

"Small hammerheads and baby whites, mostly, but you don't have to worry about them too much. They don't usually come in to feed this time of night."

"They wear watches, do they? And follow set patterns for breakfast, lunch and dinner?"

Michael leaned back in his chair and stretched out his long legs at the side of the table. He reached to an inside pocket of his jacket and withdrew a slim, gold cigar case.

"Do you mind?"

Normally, Megan found all manner of smoking an annoyance—cigarettes, pipes, and most especially cigars. But somehow here, on a rundown porch at the rear of a Bahamian greasy spoon, with the ocean threatening her ankles and a handsome man sitting opposite her in a tuxedo . . . smoking seemed entirely appropriate.

"What have you been doing with yourself all these years, Michael?" she asked.

"Surviving. And you?"

"Surviving," she echoed.

His pale blue eyes sought out her left hand. "Having come damned close to ravishing you in the parking lot, I suppose I should ask—is there a Mr. Thomas?"

"There was . . . for a while." She followed his gaze to the wide, gold wedding band she wore and twisted it self-consciously. "I wear it out of habit, and because . . . because it saves a lot of unnecessary questions and explanations. What about you?"

"I decided a long time ago, I wasn't the marrying kind." He paused and cupped his hand around a lighter, touching the blue flame to the end of his cigar. The scent of mild tobacco, sweetly tainted with bay and rum, drifted across the table and Megan found herself identifying the source of one of the heady, masculine aromas that clung to his skin and clothes.

"Children?"

Megan lifted her eyes to his. "No. No children."

"The law profession keeps you pretty busy, I guess."

"How did you know I was a lawyer?"

"A lucky guess." He grinned. "Besides, your father, grandfather and a spate of uncles were all lawyers—not to mention the Brothers Grimm. They still in politics?"

"Anthony is a junior congressman and Ryan is taking a shot at the senate this term."

Michael whistled softly. "Daddy must be quite proud."

"Father is . . . Father. He assumed my—what did you call them? My Brothers Grimm?—he *assumed* they would get where they are today. He never had any doubts about any of us."

"As long as you were heading in the direction he wanted you to head. I mean, he might not have been so effusive if you had wanted to become, say . . . a florist?"

"He wanted to see us successful," she said quietly. "There was nothing wrong with that."

"Nothing at all," he agreed, leaving his sarcasm hanging in the air between them. Before Megan could draw him out any further, George was swinging through the door, his hands balancing a tray laden with glasses and a straw-bound bottle of wine. He set his burden on the table and, with the true aplomb of a maître d', he fished a bent corkscrew out of one of his voluminous trouser pockets, put it down on the table and whistled his way back to the kitchen, leaving Michael to uncork and pour the wine.

The task completed, he raised his glass and offered a toast.

"To unfinished business."

"Unfinished?"

He took a sip of wine. "You may not have known it at the time, but it took me months to work up the nerve to ask you out on a date. You were the golden girl. Untouchable. Unattainable. Too sweet and wholesome to be sullied by...by someone like me. You had brains, too, and a kind of unpretentious class that made you stick out a country mile even when you were sweating it out in gym class, your hair all over your face, and your tight little blue bloomers stained and wrinkled. In fact, as I recall, I lost a rather heavy bet once by saying you never sweated at all."

Megan winced. "Was I that bad?"

"In the beginning? Worse. And you were dating some big blond bastard for the longest time—the captain of the football team, or some such thing. I seriously contemplated sabotaging his jockstrap...or throttling him outright...if you didn't come to your senses and dump the jerk before I had to...well, before the end of the term." He paused and his smile turned sly. "Do you remember a goofy-looking kid name Skinner? He had a nose that went from his forehead to his chin, and a reputation for having something else just as prominent."

The name sounded vaguely familiar, but Megan was too mesmerized by the sound of Michael's voice to spare more than a noncommittal shrug.

"Well, I paid him twenty bucks to introduce your captain to Breastwork Betty, hoping to hurry his natural urges along a little."

Megan's eyes widened and her chin lifted off her hand. Breastwork Betty's nickname had been well deserved, and her sudden interest in Megan's boyfriend had been grist for the school's rumor mill for weeks. The scandal had only been surpassed by Megan's appearance at the midterm party with Michael Antonacci at her side.

"You *arranged* for Bill Caulder and I to break up?"

"I wanted a clear field."

"Do you always get what you want?" she asked, oddly irritated by manipulations that had taken place so long ago.

"Most of the time." His teeth flashed whitely through the muted shadows. "Why does it make you angry? You should be flattered I went to so much trouble."

"Flattered? Because of you, I had no date to the prom. Because of you, I was grounded for a month and had to hear all about Bill and Betty making the rounds of the year-end parties. Where did you go, anyway? And why did you leave school so close to graduation?"

The humor faded visibly from Michael's eyes and he bought a moment's delay to regroup his thoughts by drawing on his cigar. "It was family business. I had been putting off making certain decisions for a few months, and, well, I just couldn't put them off any longer."

"But surely your family would have understood."

"Education was never one of their priorities, and they never did thank Father Joe for insisting I attend Fairgate. But if it will ease your mind, I not only finished high school, but earned a masters degree in business administration. Of course, if you tell anyone that, I'll categorically deny it. It's not the kind of thing we anti-establishment types like to have spread around."

Megan arched an eyebrow delicately. "It would ease my mind even more to know why you introduced yourself as Michael Vallaincourt rather than Antonacci."

"Vallaincourt was my mother's maiden name. It just seemed to fit the locale and the mood of the islands better than an Italian moniker."

"Your mother was French?"

"Born and raised in Paris. She and Pop met during the war, but they didn't get together until quite a few years later. She died when I was six years old. Ahh, here comes the food at last!"

He stubbed out his cigar just as George kicked his way through the door. This time he was carrying a wad of folded newspapers and a steaming bucket. Michael helped him spread the papers on the table, and, after cautioning Megan to guard the wineglasses, he signaled George to empty the contents of the bucket between them.

Crab legs, fat and succulent, came tumbling out of the pail onto the papers. One of the other customers, shanghaied into being an assistant, came up behind George carrying napkins, picks and metal crackers. These he deposited on the table, grumbling about not being paid to be a waiter. Then, he added two small crockery pots of sauce to the assemblage.

"This one," Michael warned, tapping a crab claw against the side of one of the pots, "is hot enough to melt the barnacles off the keel of a ship. The other isn't much better, but at least you can remember how to walk and talk afterward. You do like crab, don't you?"

He knew she did, having canceled the order of buttered crab she had selected earlier from the hotel menu.

Megan laughed as she watched him tuck a huge cloth napkin into the collar of his two-hundred-dollar shirt. The absolute contradictions in his character and mannerisms were confusing her more than ever. He looked, talked and acted with the suavity of a man accustomed to all the luxuries life could provide, yet she knew he had grown up in a two-room apartment over a fruit market. Fast cars, silk tuxedos...all of it suited the man who called himself Michael Vallaincourt, yet here he was, cracking crab legs on newspaper and licking his fingers with the relish of a longshoreman. She did not dare steal a peek under the table, but she imagined his shoes were off and his toes curled against the planking with pleasure.

Conversations flowed easily between mouthfuls, each of them dredging up their memories for anecdotes that would send the other off into gales of laughter. George brought more wine, but although Michael topped his glass as frequently as he added to Megan's he was more intoxicated by Megan's soft-lit beauty. He watched her as she talked, his attention focused alternately on her lips, or on the exotic, jade green of her eyes.

By the same token, it took a mighty effort for him not to succumb to the temptation to reach over and tuck an escaped wisp of hair back behind her ear, or to damn convention entirely and simply snatch away all the pins that were holding her hair imprisoned at her nape. He could envision what it would look like spilling around her shoulders and throat like molten gold, and he resented the tiny pearled clip and pins for taunting him.

Equally debilitating on his willpower was the combination of light from the moon and from the diner windows behind her. Together they were conspiring to shape and outline the sensuous contours of her body, luring his eye here or there as if daring him to find fault anywhere.

There were no faults. Her breasts were high and firm, the berrylike nubs of her nipples betraying the fact that there was nothing between her skin and the silky-soft jersey of her sundress. Her throat was graceful, her waist was trim and taut, her legs went on forever.

She wore little or no makeup, a refreshing change from the women he usually met. Young spoiled beauties, most of them, siliconed front and rear, every hair in place, every inch of skin buffed and glossed and presented in garish Technicolor....

"Hello? Anyone home?"

Michael blinked. "I'm sorry. My mind was a million miles away."

"It does feel odd...being together again after all these years."

He shook his head slowly. "It feels like the most natural thing in the world. Nothing about you has changed—not the way you look, not the way you laugh, not even the way you tilt your head to one side when you think someone is shooting you a line of b.s."

Megan straightened her head with an abrupt little jerk and flushed. "You haven't exactly grown fat and bald yourself, you know. And before you let the compliment swell your head, those *are* gray hairs I see, are they not?"

"Shall we adjourn into the stronger light for an eyeball-to-eyeball comparison?"

"You wouldn't find a single gray hair anywhere on my body," she said smugly.

"Not anywhere? Now there's a challenge any healthy male would be hard-pressed to refuse. Do you mind if I fetch my bifocals first?"

Megan's flush darkened. "That didn't come out the way I meant it to. You wear bifocals?"

"No," he said, grinning. "But I can see where a near-sighted man would have definite advantages."

Megan stared at him for a moment before throwing her hands up. "It's happening again, I can feel it. Look at me—am I blushing, or am I blushing?"

"You are very definitely, very attractively blushing."

"But I haven't blushed since—" she looked out over the bay and sighed "—I haven't blushed since I answered the phone that day and heard your voice on the other end asking me to go to the party with you. I deal all day long with attorneys and clients and I don't ever get flustered or tongue-tied. I never feel self-conscious. I never feel off balance. I never feel...vulnerable." She looked back and his eyes were waiting for her. "So why do I feel all those things when I am around you? I felt them fifteen years ago, and dammit, I feel them now."

"I don't know why, Meg," he said gently. "Maybe because we never got to finish what we started."

The same heated sensation that had undermined her so unexpectedly out in the parking lot, rippled through her again, catching at her breath, making her tremble.

"Or maybe it's because you were everything I couldn't have," she whispered. "You were the proverbial bad boy. You weren't afraid to tell anyone to go to hell, and you never did what anyone expected or asked you to do unless you wanted to do it. You belonged to no one but yourself, answered to no one but yourself, and . . . I guess it's just a little unsettling to find out that life hasn't changed you. It hasn't made you fat or balding or content to play ball with your twelve kids on a Sunday afternoon."

"Twelve kids?"

"Never mind," she said, shaking away both the question and the smile lurking in his eyes. "The point is, even belonging to the so-called establishment, acquiring a degree of wealth and success and influence— even that hasn't changed you. You still have a Harley, for heaven's sake."

"It keeps me grounded in reality."

"It makes you dangerous, Michael. Dangerous and intimidating to someone who has had her whole life mapped out."

He tilted his head enough to see her ankles beneath the table. "I don't see any ropes or chains."

"They're there. They always were. And there were times I felt them squeezing so tightly I could hardly breathe."

Michael's arms were crossed nonchalantly over his chest, but there was nothing casual about the tempered blue steel of his eyes. They studied her in silence, and she wanted to look away, not knowing where the words had come from, or why she had blurted them out to him of all people . . . but she couldn't avert her gaze. She wanted him to look away, to leave her failures and longings private . . . but she knew he wouldn't.

"What about your husband? Didn't he give you any kind of slack?"

"My husband? He only married me in order to wheedle his way into the family law firm. His first affair began the week after we returned from our honeymoon."

"The man was a fool," Michael said intently.

"So was I. But only that one time. And never again."

"You have that written in stone somewhere?"

"*Engraved* in it," she insisted.

Michael had seen her confusion change into anger, and part of him knew enough to tread softly, slowly. She had been badly hurt once and was making it perfectly clear she had no intention of ever being hurt again.

Yet another part of him could not suppress the wave of satisfaction that came with knowing she had no lingering tender emotions for her ex-husband. None lingering and probably none ever fully explored. It was an intriguing prospect to consider: Megan Worth, the ultimate in a man's desire for beauty and passion, never having been made to feel either. Her anger, in its present form, was only a spark away from arousal. Her passion, he had already discovered, was as close as a kiss.

What would it take, he wondered, to turn that spark into a blazing fire? How hot would her passion burn and how badly would she sear herself into his own peace of mind?

4

"IT MUST BE close to midnight," Megan managed to whisper. "Shouldn't we be leaving?"

Michael pulled himself together with a frown. "You're right, I suppose. Gino will be typing up his resignation again if I don't get back on time."

"Again? He's done it before?"

"At least once a week," Michael said, nodding wryly. "Remember those converts to the sunshine I told you about? Well, Gino isn't one of them. He misses the snow and the kamikaze races with Manhattan taxi drivers."

"Have you been friends a long time?"

His hesitation was almost too slight to notice. "Long enough. Got everything?"

Megan unslung her purse from the back of the chair and stood, not surprised to find Michael beside her, close enough for their bodies to touch.

"Are you and your cousin on any kind of heavy-duty schedule while you're here?"

Megan shook her head and smiled. "Shari's idea of a tight schedule is to plan on waking up some time during the day."

"Good. Then she won't mind if I kidnap you for dinner again tomorrow night."

"I . . . I don't know. It will depend on how she feels."

"Tempt me, and I'll arrange to slip a Mickey Finn into her afternoon rum punch."

Meg laughed. "I can't promise anything, Michael. I'll just have to see how the day goes."

"Fair enough," he conceded and hooked his hand through her arm.

They retraced their steps through the steaming obstacle course of the kitchen and paused at the counter while George's sharp eyes assessed Megan's praise for the meal. Deciding it was genuine, he beamed at hearing she had never before eaten such delicious seafood, and he made her promise to come back and try his shark steaks.

Neither one of them paid much attention to Michael as he withdrew a leather wallet and extracted a sheaf of bills. Megan probably would not have taken a second glance except that the notes he pulled out were hundred dollar bills and there had to be enough of them to total at least a thousand dollars. In a flash they had disappeared into one of George's deep pockets.

"Thanks, George," Michael was saying. "The sauce could have been a little spicier, but on the whole, it was pretty good."

"Pretty good," George snorted. "Next time, mon, I make you my own hot sauce an' we see if you can eat it without bawlin' like a baby."

"It isn't when I eat it that I cry the hardest," Michael confided with a wry grimace.

George threw his head back and laughed, a loud, long, belly-slapping laugh that followed Megan and Michael through the main dining room and out into the starlit night.

Meg was still shell-shocked over the amount of money she had just seen change hands. She was slow to feel the sudden tension in Michael's fingers as they dug into the flesh of her upper arm; slower yet in reacting to the sight of the gleaming black Mercedes sedan that was parked alongside the Ferrari.

"Good evening, Mr. Vallaincourt," a voice said from the shadows. "Your receptionist at the hotel was kind enough to tell us where we might find you."

There were three of them. Three men in dark suits who were spaced far too casually between the diner and the cars to be anything but there on a mission. The one closest—the speaker—moved forward, his shoes crunching softly over the gravel. He came to a halt in the spill of light from the door and Megan recognized him from the casino.

"Mr. Samosa would like to see you if you aren't too busy."

"Can't it wait until morning?" Michael asked, his voice a sheet of ice.

The man shrugged and eased aside his jacket to reveal a gun holstered at his waist. "As it turns out, Mr. Samosa has decided to fly back to Venezuela tonight and wants to speak with you before he leaves."

Michael's cold gaze briefly touched on all three men, flicking over them with the sharpness of a razor blade. His body was tense, communicating mixed messages to Megan through the ironlike grip of his hand. He knew these men. He did not like or trust them, however, and was not particularly enamored of accompanying them anywhere in the middle of the night.

"I guess I could spare him ten minutes. You have no objections if the lady goes back to the hotel?"

The stranger looked at Megan without interest and shrugged again. "Say good-night quickly. Oh, and—" He held out a hand as Michael started to walk past, laying it flat against the broad, tuxedoed chest. He smiled and slid his fingers beneath the jacket, pulling them out again along with a small, deadly-looking automatic. "We'll just hold on to this for you for a while, if you don't mind. You can have it back later."

The muscles along Michael's jaw tautened into a ridge and his expression turned even blacker as he hurried Megan toward the Ferrari.

"Michael, who are those men? What do they want with you? Why were you carrying a *gun?*" The last question echoed the shocking realization that he had been wearing it all night as he'd sat across from her.

"Can you drive a stick?"

"A stick shift? Yes, but—"

"Good. Take the car back to the hotel—do you think you can find your way back again? Turn left onto the highway and follow it straight into Freeport. You shouldn't have any problem once you're there. Just ask anyone for directions."

"Michael . . . I can't drive your car!"

"You don't have much choice," he said bluntly. "Don't worry, you'll be fine."

"Michael, who are those men? Where are they taking you? Should I call the police?"

He took a deep breath to calm himself, but looked as if he would have preferred shaking her. "No. I don't want you to call the police. I don't want you do anything but get into the car and drive back to the Privateer. I know these men. They work for a business associate of mine who sleeps by day and works by night. Everything is all right, These three—" he gestured over his shoulder "—are paid extra to look and act like morons."

"But, Michael—"

He kissed her, hard and fast, and urged her to one side so he could open the door of the Ferrari.

"Michael!"

"Get in. Go back to the hotel, go straight to your bungalow and get a good night's sleep. I'll come by in the morning and take you to breakfast."

Megan glanced past his shoulder. The three men were now standing by the Mercedes. The one who had spoken earlier appeared to be amusing himself by examining Michael's gun. He must have sensed her eyes on him, for he looked over and grinned, the unpleasant ugliness of his expression sending a wave of revulsion shivering clean through to Megan's toes. Michael felt her reaction, and if it was possible for his mood to grow bleaker, it did.

"I'll explain everything tomorrow," he promised, and coaxed her into the Ferrari. Once she was settled behind the wheel, he buckled the seat belt, fed the key into the ignition and pushed the various buttons on the dash that brought the interior and exterior lights bursting to life.

"Should I . . . should I at least find Gino and tell him what has happened?"

Michael studied the smooth oval of her face for a moment, then bent to kiss her again.

"Do exactly what I told you to do," he murmured against her lips. "Go to your room, lock the door and stay there until morning."

On impulse, Megan flung her arms around his neck and dragged his mouth back down to hers, kissing him with all the urgency and desperation she was feeling. Michael's response shone from his eyes when he finally straightened. She could see the promise reflected in their silvery-blue depths, and she could hear it echoed in the parting whisper, barely audible above the whine of the idling engine.

"Tomorrow."

"Michael, please—"

"Go. Now. I want to see you drive away."

Megan moved a trembling hand to the stick shift. She found the clutch with her left foot and depressed it to the boards, then worked the clutch and the shift in tandem to ease the big red machine into reverse.

"Don't be afraid of it," Michael commanded. "Treat it like you would a lover—gently but firmly. You'll do all right."

She overrevved the engine only slightly sliding it into first gear, and by the second shift, she was in the laneway and heading out toward the main road. The last glimpse she had of Michael was through the rearview mirror. He was standing where she had left him, his hands jammed into his pockets, his body bathed in the soft red glow of the Ferrari's taillights.

5

WITH TEN different scenarios playing out in her mind, Megan was precariously close to panic by the time she wheeled the Ferrari into the parking lot of the Privateer's Paradise. She had waged war with her instincts and her lawyer's sense of outrage every speeding mile of the way. Both screamed at her to drive directly to the nearest police station and report what had happened.

Men with guns had taken Michael away. He had tried to calm her by saying it was the normal, if eccentric behavior of a business associate, but she had seen the tension in his face. She had felt it in his body, tasted it on his lips. Tension and anger. A dark, dangerous anger she had seen too many times throughout her years of criminal law to dismiss lightly.

Who was Samosa and why was he insisting on a late-night meeting? She thought back over the snatches of conversation she had overheard in the casino between the two men, and she remembered Michael's anger over a supposed discrepancy in commissions—but commissions for what? What was Samosa selling and who was buying? Both men had implied they could come to no final agreement until they had made calls to their respective clients. Were they both middlemen, then, and was Michael's client Vincent Giancarlo?

Could there be a foundation for Hornsby's suspicions or was she just letting her imagination run rampant?

Unfortunately, it did not take imagination to see that the casino would be the perfect cover for laundering money. Thousands of dollars went through the dealers' hands every day, millions each year. Money from any source could come through one door and leave by another spanking-clean and untraceable.

Another nagging question: Who was George Samson and why had Michael given him so much money?

Megan stirred and realized she was still sitting in the parked Ferrari. The luminous clock on the dash had throbbed 12:15 the last time she had noticed—fifteen minutes past the time Gino Romani expected Michael to return to the casino.

What should she do?

Despite Michael's adamant instructions that she return to her bungalow and do nothing until morning, Megan knew she could not obey. And although it went against all her instincts, she also knew she could not go to the local police, either. Whatever Michael was involved in, she doubted very much if the laid-back island bobbies could help him, or even if he would appreciate their interference.

That left only one alternative.

Megan hurried from the parking lot into the lobby of the hotel. She bypassed the reception desk and followed the tall row of marble columns to the arched entrance of the casino. Flushed from her haste, she approached the first tuxedoed security man she saw—

identified as such by the small badge on his lapel—and
asked where she might find Gino Romani.

"Mr. Romani? He went off duty at midnight, ma'am.
Can I be of any help?"

"He . . . went off duty?" Meg had not anticipated this
and she blinked stupidly at the guard.

"Yes, ma'am. In fact, he left a little early tonight, but
he'll be back on the job at noon tomorrow. If you don't
care to wait—"

She did not hear the rest of what the guard said. She
turned and ran back through the lobby. She pushed her
way through a logjam of sauntering guests, cursing
under her breath as they shouted drunken chastise-
ments after her. There were two amorous couples seated
by the pool, taking advantage of the heavy shadows,
but they couldn't have cared less if it was a tornado
blowing its way past and heading for bungalow four.

The key, naturally, was lost at the bottom of her
purse and Megan uttered an oath that would have made
Phil Levy proud. She found it finally and slotted it into
the lock, then pushed the door open to an unexpected
flare of bright lights.

Shari was perched on one of the floral-printed
couches, her mop of red hair freshly washed and
moussed, her makeup picture-perfect. She was wearing one of Megan's silk muumuus, artfully draped to
reveal a good deal more of the plunging neckline than
the designer intended.

"Why, Megan, you're back! Did you have a good
dinner? Gino has been telling me all about George's
restaurant and says we will have to make a point of going there. Maybe all four of us together." She smiled

brightly and batted her lashes, and Megan could only stare from one couch to the other; from Shari's relaxed, curled-up position in one corner, to Gino Romani's jacketless presence opposite her.

"Miz Worth," he said, rising abruptly to his feet. "I hope you don't mind. I was around earlier to check on Shar... Miss Stevenson, that is, and, well, we got to talking and—"

"And I invited him back from a drink after he finished work. Don't look so scandalized, Meg, we have kept the table between us."

"Mr. Romani, I'm glad you're here," Megan managed to say through her surprise. "I stopped in at the casino looking for you, and they told me you would not be back until tomorrow."

"You were looking for me?"

"Yes, I . . ." She hesitated and glanced at Shari. "Mr. Romani, may I talk to you for a moment in private? It's important."

Gino responded to the urgency in her voice and delayed only long enough to retrieve his jacket as he walked toward the door. Putting it on seemed to reinstate him in the role of head of security, and with a brusque nod to Shari's openmouthed astonishment, he followed Megan out onto the moonlit pathway.

"Mr. Romani—" Megan turned, too impatient to go more than a few steps "—I thought you should know . . . something has happened to Michael. We were leaving George's and there were some men there waiting for him. Three men, and they all had guns. Michael had a gun, too, but they took it away from him and—"

"Hold it! Hold it!" Gino commanded. "Slow down, Miz Worth and start again. Are you saying three men attacked Mr. Vallaincourt with guns?"

"They didn't attack, not exactly, but they were waiting for us when we came out of the restaurant. I only saw one gun, but I know they all had them. They just *looked* like they had them, if you know what I mean."

"Yeah, I know what you mean. So you were coming out of George's and they stopped you in the lot?"

Was the man deaf, or slow? "Yes. They were waiting for us in the parking lot. I think I saw one of them at the casino earlier tonight. He was with the short, Latin-looking man Michael and you were talking to. Samosa, I think his name was."

"Samosa?" Gino's heavyset features frowned for the few seconds it took him to mouth a silent oath. "What did Michael do?"

"Excuse me?"

Gino rephrased the question. "Did he act like he was going to go with them willingly, or did he try to put a couple of them nose-down in the gravel before they convinced him to join them?"

Megan looked aghast. "This is hardly a trifling matter, Mr. Romani. I was so worried I nearly ran the Ferrari off the road half a dozen times getting back here!"

"He let you drive the Ferrari?" Gino's eyes widened with surprise.

"Neither of us had much choice," she snapped coldly. "And what difference does it make if I drove it or not? Shouldn't you be more concerned about what happened to *him* rather than the damned car?"

Gino rubbed his chin thoughtfully with a hamlike hand. "Miz Worth . . . if Mikey didn't know those guys and if he didn't especially want to go anywhere with them, he'd've left them flat-out on the ground and he'd be standing here with you now."

"But they had guns!"

"Everyone on the island has a gun. It's the ones who don't, you have to worry about. And I know Samosa. He's worth a couple of bucks, so he thinks he needs bodyguards wherever he goes. But they're just glorified messengers who get paid to look mean and grunt a lot."

"That was what Michael said," Megan said slowly.

"There, you see? No problem." He grinned and looked very much like a large, handsome teddy bear. "Now, what did Michael say he wanted you to do? What did he say *exactly?*"

"He said . . . he told me to come back to the hotel."

"And?"

"And . . . to get a good night's sleep. He'd explain everything in the morning."

"He didn't tell you to come looking for me?"

"No. No, he didn't. I suggested it, but—"

"But he told you to go back to your room and not to worry."

"Yes, but—"

"Then I think you should do what he told you to do. Look, if he said he'd be here to explain everything in the morning, he'll be here."

Megan was not convinced. Still feeling anxious, she twisted and untwisted the slender leather strap of her purse.

"Miz Worth," Gino said gently. "Mikey is a big boy. He knows how to take care of himself. And this isn't the first time his plans for the evening have been interrupted. It goes with the job. The Privateer isn't the only casino on the island, either, and some of these guys—the high rollers, you know?—keep weird hours. They have breakfast in the afternoon and dinner at four in the morning, with business hours anywhere and everywhere in between. Samosa's been buzzing around here for a couple of days now, getting on everyone's nerves, especially Michael's." He laid a reassuring hand on Megan's arm. "Don't worry. Like I said, if he told you he'll see you in the morning, he'll see you in the morning. As for me, it looks like I'll have to go back and work a few extra hours in the casino. You'll explain to Miss Stevenson for me?"

Megan nodded, too numb, too bewildered, and too angry to trust herself to speak.

Gino left her standing alone on the gravel pathway. A few minutes later, when Megan returned to the bungalow, Shari was still sitting on the sofa, the muumuu discreetly rearranged to display most of her gracefully folded legs.

"Oh." She was disappointed. "He didn't come back with you?"

"He had to go back to the casino, but he sends his apologies."

"Damn! Isn't he just the dreamiest hunk you've ever seen? He's got shoulders a girl could die for...and *muscles!*"

Megan crossed in front of her cousin and threw herself in the seat Gino had recently vacated. "I take it you're feeling better?"

"I've always said the best cure for what ails you is a good man."

Megan leaned her head back, wincing when the knot of her hair intruded on her comfort. She reached around and unfastened the pearl clip, then began pulling out pins, one at a time, until the thick golden skein sprang free. Unfettered, her hair tumbled halfway down her back, a sleek blond cascade that was shaken and tousled into further disarray by fingers eager to massage the tightness out of her scalp.

"I gather something happened to spoil your date with Michael?" Shari guessed.

The massaging fingers stopped. "It was *not* a date. We met by accident in the restaurant and he suggested we go somewhere to eat."

"Somewhere other than a restaurant? How original."

"He had some business to take care of."

"At George's?"

"At George's, yes," Megan repeated quietly. Several hundred dollars worth of business. Had she missed something at the diner? An exchange of some kind? No. Michael had remained in plain sight all evening. She would have noticed if any packages had changed hands.

"For someone who enjoys her privacy so much," Shari commented dryly, "you certainly are getting around. Or was Gino an old high school flame, as well?"

"What?" Megan passed a hand wearily over her eyes. "Oh. No. Michael introduced us earlier in the evening. I needed to talk to someone and, well, he was the first person I thought of."

"What am I, boiled cabbage?

"I meant, someone connected to the resort. I'm sorry if I interrupted your tête-à-tête."

Shari's decision to pout changed to concern when she saw how troubled Megan was.

"Two heads are sometimes better than one, you know," she offered. "I may not be earmarked for the attorney general's office some day, but I do know a thing or two about unraveling plot lines and solving mysteries. And since my mind often seems to work in completely opposite directions to yours, maybe I can help."

Megan chewed thoughtfully on her lip. She knew she would eventually have to tell her cousin the whole story, but for now, maybe it would be enough just to make sense out of tonight's incident.

"All right, Shari, or should I say Constance, suppose your hero and heroine were having a pleasant dinner at a small seafood diner . . ."

She talked Shari through the meal, the easy conversation, the safe reminiscences. Her cousin's reaction to the wad of hundred dollar bills was the same as Megan's had been—astonishment. But her response to the story of the three men waiting in the parking lot was, oddly enough, closer to Gino's.

"He must have known them if he agreed to go with them."

"They had guns! Am I the only one around here who finds the notion of being forced to accompany some thugs at gunpoint somewhat appalling, not to mention the fact that what they were doing was illegal?"

"It's the lawyer in you, Megan dear. Plus the fact that you live in cushy uptown Manhattan where guns are only considered a tacky accessory at best. You should visit Queens more often. But getting back to Michael, if there really was something nasty and underhanded going on, why would those thugs—your word, not mine—agree to let you come back here? Two hostages are better than one, and if they didn't want to take you along as a hostage, you sure wouldn't have been left behind as a witness. Obviously, they weren't too concerned, so—" she spread her hands wide "—you must have been just an extra pair of eyes and ears that no one wanted around while they were discussing whatever business deal they were about to discuss. Make sense?"

Megan rubbed her temples. Unfortunately, it did make a convoluted kind of sense. If those men intended to harm Michael, they most definitely would not have let her drive away unscathed. She supposed it *could* just have been business.

"Disappointing, isn't it, to think of a great plot line only to have it fizzle out before your very eyes."

"I wouldn't say I was exactly disappointed," Megan retorted, scowling.

"Are you going to meet him in the morning?"

"I suppose I'll have to, I have his car keys."

"Are you going to have dinner with him again tomorrow night if he asks you?"

Megan jerked her head up in surprise. "I most certainly am not!"

"Not even if his explanation is boringly reasonable?"

"Not even if he leaves me gasping with awe."

"If a man made me gasp with anything short of asthma, I wouldn't be so quick to dismiss him. In fact—" she glanced conspiratorially at the half-empty glass of wine Gino had left on the table "—Gino says there is a big party in the grand ballroom tomorrow night, and he . . . well, he asked me if I was planning on going. It's a rock and roll dance, and you know I like rock music about as much as I like dried prunes, but if you're going to be in a major sulk over all this . . ."

"I am not sulking. I was worried. I still am worried, in spite of your theories and deductions. As for Gino, I am not your keeper. You can do whatever you want with whomever you want."

"Mmm. I recognize that tone of voice as the one you use on juries when you're urging them to call for the death penalty."

"You have no idea how I argue when I want the death penalty," Megan said grimly. "And I'm not trying to urge you to do or not do anything. I'm tired. I've been through hell this past hour, so if I sound a little sulky, I'm sorry."

Shari watched her cousin's face retreat behind a mask of concern.

"He'll be all right, Meg. You'll see him in the morning and he'll explain everything to you just like he promised. Naturally, I will expect you to then explain everything to me. It sounds like a terrific premise for a romantic mystery."

"In your dreams, *Constance*," Megan threatened.

"Yes, well, unfortunately, that's where I usually meet my most dashing heroes. Until now, that is. I'm thinking this situation has some very real possibilities. Very real indeed."

6

MEGAN COULDN'T SLEEP all night. She fell asleep just as the sun was levering a bleary eye over the horizon, which was about the same time she decided she had wasted enough time staring up at the ceiling. She woke a couple of hours later, twice the worse for wear, her head pounding and her nerves grating with the sounds of laughter and early-morning swimmers.

The numbers on the clock changed from 8:15 to 8:16 between her groans. She struggled out of bed and pulled on a thin bathrobe. After fighting with a knot in the belt for several seconds, she slid open the patio doors to admit the bright glare of sunlight.

Their private terrace stretched the width of the bungalow and was enclosed in a semicircle of dwarf palm trees. Beyond that was a length of shaded beach populated by taller palms and clumps of wispy sea oats. Past the stand of tall palms, a strip of sand laid out an inviting pink anvil for sunbathers. The more hearty swam and snorkeled in the crystal-clear water of the bay, the ocean beyond keeping the temperature a degree above frigid.

Megan leaned against the doorjamb and wondered for the hundredth time what she was doing here and how she had managed to be talked into helping Hornsby atone for his department's inefficiency. Why should she have to be the one to reveal Michael's real name to the justice department? And where was he? What had happened last night? Where had those men taken him? *What was he involved in, and how deep was his involvement?*

A movement drew Megan's attention to the beach. A small boy was crying. He had tripped and stubbed his toe on a root, and the fall had made him drop the armload of newspapers he had been carrying down to the beachside hut. A man in shorts and a tank top reached over and scooped the boy to his feet, brushing the sand off the thin brown legs and gently rubbing the bruised toe until the boy's choked sniffles gave way to a beaming white smile. Together, the man and boy collected the scattered papers. A final parting word and a shiny silver coin sent the boy skipping off toward the beach; the man, whose identity had been obscured by the brilliant backdrop of the water behind him, folded his paper under his arm and started walking through the palm trees in the direction of Megan's patio.

It was Michael. Very much alive and healthy, looking as if he had just vaulted off the pages of a fitness magazine.

His hair was still damp from a morning shower. Black and sleek, it was combed straight back from his forehead and tucked behind his ears. The tank top he wore was as red as his Ferrari, impressively contrasting with the deep tanned shade of his skin. His muscular physique, only hinted at beneath the silk tuxedo, was causing a flurry of turned heads and lowered sunglasses. Megan herself found she was holding her breath and gripping the metal edge of the sliding door for support.

"Good morning," he called. He slipped off his sunglasses and squinted up at the sky. "It looks like we're in for another hellish day in paradise."

"Good morning," Megan replied calmly. "I suppose you have come for your car keys?"

He paused a mere half beat before smiling. "Actually, no. But I do seem to recall having made a breakfast date with you. Here is your paper, the coffee will be along in a few minutes."

Megan ignored the newspaper he held out to her, or did she return his smile. However, instead of savaging his sunny disposition, as intended, her aloofness only caused his grin to broaden. His eyes gleamed appreciatively, as well, taking full advantage of the breeze's generosity in outlining the curves of Megan's body. Her nightgown and wrap were both made of thin polished satin and surrendered to the teasing breaths of wind without much of a protest. Her hair was long and loose, flowing around her shoulders much the way Michael had envisioned it last night, and the effect of it on his senses cost him a few moments of hard concentration.

"I know it's an old line," he mused. "But has anyone ever told you you're beautiful when you're angry?"

"I'm not angry. Why should I be angry?"

"Oh…and this is just a wild guess, mind you…but I'd say you were a little peeved over what happened last night."

"According to you and the rest of the world, *nothing* happened last night. And I wasn't peeved," she said succinctly. "I was worried sick."

"You shouldn't have been. I told you there was nothing to be concerned about. It was a business meeting. Arranged in a rather unorthodox manner, I'll admit, but in my line of work, you run into some fairly unorthodox characters."

"What exactly *is* your line of work, Michael?"

The teal blue eyes narrowed slightly. "Entrepreneur and rampant capitalist. Anything illegal in that, Counselor?"

"Not if that's *all* you do," she said bluntly. She was suffering from a lack of sleep and a glaring lack of contrition on Michael's part, and the two combined to fan her temper a degree higher. "In *my* line of work, men who attend business meetings in the company of gun-toting gorillas are not usually conducting transactions that can be reported in the *Wall Street Journal*."

He studied her expression for a long moment. "I see. And by association, you assumed I am one of these gun-toting gorillas, too?"

"If the shoe fits . . . ?"

Michael very slowly, very deliberately folded the arms of his sunglasses and hooked them over the neckline of his tank top. As he did so, his hand flexed and the signet ring caught a ray of sunlight, flashing it back into Megan's eyes.

"If I didn't know better," he said quietly, "I would think you were accusing me of something."

"I'm sorry if it seems that way. Increased curiosity is a natural by-product of my job. It is a hard habit to break, even when I'm on vacation."

"Are you? On vacation, I mean."

A flush of heat swept through Megan's body, staining her cheeks a shade too dark to go unnoticed. Seeing it, Michael was momentarily caught off guard, for he had only been taking a shot in the dark. He had not expected the shot to backfire.

The change that came over his face was one of the most unpleasant things Megan had ever had to witness. All the warmth and easy camaraderie vanished. His eyes took on the look and chill of a glacier, and his mouth hardened to a forbidding slash. She could sense him going back over their previous day's conversations, searching for clues he had missed, mistakes he might have made. It was then that Megan believed him capable of doing almost anything.

"If . . . if you'll wait a second, I'll get your keys," she stammered, anxious to break the icy hold of his eyes.

"Don't bother," he snapped. "You can just drop them off in the lobby when you get a chance."

They both started slightly at the sound of footsteps rushing toward them across the sand, but it was only the little boy he had helped earlier, his hands balancing a small tray.

"Here comes Rickey with your coffee. You'll forgive me if I don't join you. I find if I drink it too early in the morning, it gives me a sour disposition for the rest of the day."

With that, he left. The casual, sauntering stride that had brought him up from the beach was transformed into a brisk step that swallowed the distance from the patio to the gravel pathway in a few angry seconds.

Megan's brief flirtation with panic gave way to a heated surge of resentment. She glared at the boy while he set the coffee tray on the patio table. She did not reply to his cheerful greeting, but sent him scrambling back to the safety of the beach, instead, as she stepped into her room and slammed the sliding door closed behind her.

She went directly to her dresser and yanked open the top drawer. There, in the company of the few bits and pieces of jewelry Megan had brought on the trip, was the plain gold bracelet Hornsby had given her to wear.

Picking the bracelet up, she held it in the palm of her hand and compared the weight of her conscience to the weight of sentiment. Fifteen years was a long time. People changed. It was obvious Michael had changed from the young man who had tried so hard to convince her he was not cut from the same cloth as his neighborhood peers, to...what? What was Michael? A thug? A criminal?

It was easy to get caught up in a web of power and money and greedy ambition; easier still for a rebel and nonconformist to thumb his nose at society and take up where his father had left off.

In the casino last night, Megan had noticed the signet ring Michael wore, and had remembered vaguely that it had a story behind it. A few moments ago the memory had returned with alarming clarity.

Nickolaus Antonacci had been a local leader of the teamster's union in the early sixties, a position and a union that had been linked with organized crime since the early days of Prohibition. He had been gunned down in an alleyway one night, and, although the story itself had made very small headlines, his successor—

Vincent Giancarlo—had certainly gone on to much bigger and better things.

Would it be so outlandish to suppose Giancarlo would feel a certain kinship with the son of his closest friend? Moreover, where would Michael's loyalties lie—with a system that treated him like a rebel and an outcast? Or with a family that would have welcomed his cleverness and daring with open arms?

Megan smoothed her fingertips over the dull surface of the bracelet. Whether Michael was involved or not, guilty of any wrongdoing or not, it was not for her to decide. He had made his choice and seemed content enough to live with it. Unfortunately, she was not so lucky.

She had no choice at all.

7

"YOU HAVE to decide now," Shari insisted. "Either we both go the party, or we both stay here in the bungalow and count the flowers on the wallpaper."

"I don't want to go to the party," Megan said calmly. "I am not in a party mood."

"But it's a rock and roll party, with old music and funny bands in slicked-back hair and white buck shoes. It'll be fun!"

"I thought you loathed rock and roll music."

"It certainly isn't my favorite," Shari admitted with aplomb, "but I don't *loathe* it."

"You likened it to your fondness for dried prunes."

"Prunes are a necessary evil sometimes."

"So go and enjoy yourself. I'm not stopping you."

Shari scowled and crossed her arms over her chest. "Fine. Go ahead—ruin my entire vacation."

"We've only been here two days. It is hardly an entire vacation."

"It is if you've spent one of those two days clinging to life over a toilet bowl instead of touring the nightlife in a red Ferrari."

Megan went in search of the aspirin. "I went to the straw market with you this morning, didn't I? I ate conch chowder and sunburned my nose on the beach with you this afternoon, didn't I? I just came back from sharing an incredibly decadent lobster dinner with you . . . how much more togetherness do you want? Besides, I thought you had a hot date with Gino tonight?"

"I don't have a date. Not exactly, anyway. He only mentioned that he would be working in the ballroom tonight instead of the casino, and if I happened to be there, he might possibly be able to find the time to buy me a drink."

Megan swallowed two aspirin and glared at her cousin over the rim of the water glass. "So why do you need me there? You are hardly anyone's idea of a wall-flower."

"I don't want to go alone," Shari said stubbornly. "I don't want him to think I have nothing better to do than sit around waiting for him to find the time to buy me a drink."

Megan groaned. "What about the group of party animals you met on the beach today? Are none of them going?"

Shari looked horrified. "I don't want it to look like I'm going with a date! What's more, those party animals, as you call them, wouldn't ask me to go with them for fear *you* might tag along. Honestly, Meg, you were downright obnoxious this afternoon. Just because your knickers are in a twist over whatever Michael did or did not say to you that did or did not meet with your approval, you didn't have to take it out on us by snarling and barking at everyone who dared impinge on your private space."

"I did not snarl. And my—what? Knickers?—are not in a twist over anyone or anything."

"Good. Then you'll come to the party?"

Megan opened her mouth to argue, but closed it again without saying a word. It would be easier just to agree, to go to the damned party long enough for Shari to find a friendly face. Then, having done her duty, Megan could exit discreetly and return to the peace and sanctity of her own company.

"All right. If it will make you happy, I'll go. But you will owe me a big one, cousin of mine, like a snorkeling trip along the reef tomorrow."

Shari's expression of triumph faltered briefly. She loved being in the water almost as much as she loved being in the sky. Balancing the scale on the other end, however, was the muscular swarthiness of Gino Romani, and her decision was made on a smug nod. "Deal. I'll be ready in five minutes."

Megan moved at a less enthusiastic pace, cursing inwardly as she selected a dress from the closet. She settled on one that was such a pale green, it was almost white. The top was a form-hugging bandeau with spaghetti straps. As she adjusted the folds of the skirt, the gold bracelet she wore reflected glints of light in the mirror.

A touch of hair spray smoothed the tendrils that had escaped the tightly coiled chignon. A dab of perfume on her throat revitalized her enough to put on a determined smile as she responded to Shari's impatient shout from the sitting room.

Her cousin's dress of garish pink flowers suited the tropical mood of the island. She wore several ropes of seashells around her neck and more on her wrists, and had swept back the riot of red curls at her temple, taming them with two large cloisonné combs.

She eyed Megan's effortless elegance with a cryptic frown.

"You look like you're dressed for a wild night at the symphony."

"I can always change back into a bathrobe," Megan warned.

"I hear the snorkeling is terrific."

They both laughed and left the bungalow, walking the short distance to the main building arm in arm. Just outside the swinging doors, Megan was halted by the sight of a large freckled hand reaching swiftly in front of her to grab the door.

"Well, howdy there, Miss Megan," said Dallas jovially. "Are y'all aimin' to try your luck at the tables again tonight?"

"I don't think so," Megan said with a wry smile. "I believe I have used up my allotment of luck for one vacation."

"Bah! Y'all will change your mind before your two weeks are over—you did say you were stayin' two weeks, didn't you? Well, hell, that's plenty o' time to get bit by the bug again. And if'n you do, you know where to find me. Same seat, same table."

Not the same good luck charm, Megan realized as she glanced at the leggy blonde attached to Dallas's arm. Lucy evidently hadn't been enough of a talisman to earn the right to stand by his side two nights in a row.

Dallas left them waiting for the glass elevators. The main ballroom was on the second floor, and, as Megan watched Dallas hurrying off toward the entrance of the casino, the elevator arrived and she was moved forward with the crush of bodies.

"He was kind of cute, if you like lecherous old men," Shari murmured in her ear. "Lecherous *rich* old men, I might add. Did you see the size of the rock on his pinkie ring? Two carats if it's a point."

Megan smiled tightly and toyed with the gold band around her wrist. She had noted the attention of several men as she'd walked through the lobby, and more this afternoon on the beach. Had the right person noticed the bracelet and would he—or she—be making contact soon? Megan had worn the bracelet all day, and as the hours progressed, the weight of it seemed to have increased proportionately. She had already decided that the moment she had fulfilled her part of the bargain, she and Shari would leave the hotel. She did not think she could get Shari onto another plane so soon, but she was sure she could think of a reasonable excuse to change hotels, preferably to one on the far side of the island.

The ballroom was not as large or cavernous as the casino, nor nearly as grand as the word implied, but there was the obligatory revolving ball of cut mirrors suspended from the middle of the ceiling, and a raised stage at one end to support the various bands as they performed. Tables surrounded a huge dance floor, most of them occupied already. Couples who were still sitting were watching the gyrations of others who were dancing to an old Chubby Checker tune.

"Isn't this great!" Shari cried.

"Great," Megan grumbled.

They found an empty table—close to a rear door, Megan noted with relief—and ordered drinks from the ponytailed waitress. When she returned with her tray a few minutes later, she deposited the glasses, but waved away the money Megan withdrew from her purse.

"No charge, ladies. Boss says it's on the house."

Megan followed the waitress's glance and felt an instant tightness in her throat.

Michael was standing in the doorway. He looked exactly as he had the night before, his black tuxedo making him stand out from the men in their flowered shirts and white pants.

"That's Michael?" Shari gasped. She clutched Megan's arm with enough vehemence to dig her nails into the tender flesh. "*That's* Michael? He's *gorgeous!*"

Megan averted her head quickly. She did not want to speak to him. She did not want that sickly, off-balance feeling to cloud her judgment any more than it had already. She gave the gold bracelet another twist and desperately gauged the distance between their table and the rear door.

"He's coming this way," Shari warned. "My God, he even walks gorgeously."

Megan stood up, promptly knocking her purse onto the floor. In her haste to scoop it up, the clasp popped open and the contents scattered around her feet.

"Damn, damn, damn," she muttered under her breath. She grabbed, snatched and scrabbled after coins and sunglasses, and what seemed to her to be the entire contents of a Pandora's box.

When she straightened, she could tell by the rapt look on Shari's face that her haste had been in vain.

"Good evening, ladies."

Shari's mouth fell open and Megan's eyes closed.

If she says "Hello, gorgeous," I'll smack her, Megan thought wildly. I swear I will.

"Enjoying yourselves, I hope?" Michael's eyes flicked to Shari and he smiled. "You must be Miss Stevenson. Megan told me you were feeling under the weather yesterday. I see you managed to get some sun today."

Shari's blush spread to the roots of her hair, but she recovered enough of her wits to return his smile. "We had a great day, thank you. Your hotel is terrific."

Michael accepted the compliment with a slight nod. "If you wouldn't mind, I'd like to steal Megan away for a dance. I managed to sneak out of the casino for a few minutes, but I'm sure they'll have the bloodhounds out looking for me any time now."

Shari waved her hand absently. "I don't mind at all. Take her for as long as you like. In fact, I was just sitting here to keep her company for a while until some other friends arrived, and gosh, would you look at that, there they are now."

"*Shari!*" Megan could hardly believe her ears.

Immune to green daggers, Shari stood and made a show of waving to someone across the room before she gathered up her drink and her purse. In the process, she leaned close enough to Megan's ear to hiss, "Let your hair down, for heaven's sake. You aren't in court now."

Megan stared after her, watching the cap of red curls weave between the tables. When she turned back to Michael, there was a dark gleam of amusement in his eyes, and, before she could protest, he took her gently by the arm and drew her easily, expertly into his embrace as the musicians began to play a Righteous Brothers tune.

Megan was still partially in shock. She managed to remain tense and unyielding through the first half of the song, but then the melody and lyrics of "Unchained Melody" began to work in conspiracy with the heat and closeness of Michael's body, and she felt herself succumbing, her resolutions dissolving along with the stiffness in her spine.

"You don't play fair, Mr. Vallaincourt," she said accusingly.

"If there is a choice between playing fair and winning, I prefer to win every time."

He was too close and he smelled too good—a warm, heady blend of maleness, sun and aromatic tobacco. His hand was too firm where it pressed into the small of her back. His heartbeat was too near her own.

"I wanted to apologize for my behavior this morning," he said quietly. "I was rude and there was no excuse for it."

"You have nothing to apologize for," Megan countered. "If anything, I should be the one apologizing to you. I said some things I should never have said. I...was angry, and upset, and...and I shouldn't have said them."

"No, you shouldn't have assumed the roles of judge and jury. But you had a right to be angry. I owed you a better explanation than the one I gave you."

Megan closed her eyes, wishing fervently that his mouth was not so near her ear as he was speaking. Each word sent tiny melting reverberations flowing down her spine. There, they pooled and shimmered until the pleasure was almost too much to bear.

"You . . . don't owe me anything," she whispered.

"Yes. I do."

His arm tightened around her waist and Megan groaned inwardly, fighting the weakness, fighting the temptation. She tried to focus on the other dancers moving sinuously around them, but that did more harm than good. She looked up at the sparks of light bouncing off the facets of the mirrored globe, but they were too much like the sparks showering through her body. It was no use. The more she resisted the heat, the hotter the flames grew. The more she tried to ignore the sensations tingling throughout her body, the more her flesh ached for a more poignant intimacy.

Michael felt the tremors shivering through her and he took shameful advantage. He curled his hand more possessively around hers and lifted it so that his lips had access to the wildly beating pulse at her wrist. He heard her gasp and only had to turn his head fractionally to capture that same gasp beneath his lips. He drew her closer, holding her so that their bodies molded together, and she knew she was not alone in her weakness and need.

His mouth was bold and relentless, his kiss as electrifying as the lights and music that blazed around them. Yet they could have been alone on the dance floor for all the effect the surrounding distractions made. And when the kiss ended, her mouth, her heart, her entire being quaked with a desire she had not felt in fifteen years.

"Megan . . . ?"

It was all she could do to open her eyes and look up at him.

"Megan, if I asked you to come home with me tonight, would you do it?"

"Home?" The word sounded thick and fuzzy on her tongue; just saying it drained her remaining reserves of strength.

"Megan . . . I promise I will answer all your questions, offer all explanations owed . . . but not tonight. Tonight, I don't want to talk at all."

Megan moaned softly as his mouth covered hers again. The melting sensation spread with alarming force and she had to wrap her arm tightly around his neck to keep her knees from buckling beneath her. She knew how shameless she appeared, how easily swayed by the mere press of flesh . . . but she didn't care. She didn't want to live out her life as an ice queen. She was flesh and blood and emotion, and by God, so was Michael. In the morning she could weather the storm of guilt and recriminations. In the morning she could let her conscience wag its finger. For now . . . for now, she just wanted this. She wanted Michael. She wanted his heat and his passion, and she wanted him to teach her how to set that same heat and passion free within herself.

Michael cursed against her lips as he lowered his hand from her waist, the fingers stroking down her hip and thigh, skimming upward again with the hem of her skirt in tow.

"Say yes," he growled huskily. "Say you will come home with me now, or I swear I'll take you here and now, before God *and* the Righteous Brothers."

"Yes," she gasped. "Yes, Michael. Yes."

His gaze studied her intently, searching for any sign of pretense. What he saw, however, was an arousal so intense, it scalded his senses and sent a primitive, unholy heat coursing through his veins.

The music ended and Michael eased her to arm's length. She was mildly startled to see that he had maneuvered them to within steps of the exit.

"I'll . . . just tell Shari . . ."

He shook his head. "No. I mean to kidnap you properly this time. Maybe in a few hours I'll let you use a phone, or—" his eyes lowered and settled hungrily on the lush moistness of her lips "—maybe not."

"What about you? The casino?"

"The casino will get along just fine without me."

He took her hand in his and, with a glance over his shoulder, he ushered her through the door and down a steep flight of stairs.

What she was doing—what they both were doing was madness. Sheer and utter madness! There were fifteen years worth of changes in their lives, and they still lived and worked on very opposite sides of the tracks, yet Megan did not care. She felt the years and the pressures of her responsibilities being swept away on the cool, tropical breeze.

She settled into the deep seat of the Ferrari with a giddy sense of freedom. She was only dimly aware of the passing noise and traffic as they drove out of Freeport; she had no idea if they'd traveled one mile or twenty, ten minutes or an hour before the car slowed and prowled onto the fine gravel of a long, winding driveway.

A small, whitewashed beach house emerged from the darkness, its windows reflecting the harsh glare of the Ferrari's headlights.

"My seaside retreat," Michael announced. "Keep in mind I live alone, so if you're a neat freak, you'll have to keep your eyes closed."

He cut the engine and the house disappeared into the blackness again. With the car silenced, Megan could hear the rustle of palm trees and the sound of waves lapping onto a nearby shore.

She let herself be helped out of the car and was dismayed to discover her legs were no stronger than when she'd left the resort. She was grateful for his arm around her waist and grateful for the darkness that shielded the warm flush in her cheeks.

"Two steps," he cautioned, abandoning her briefly while he found the right key on his ring and fit it to the lock.

Not exactly sure what to expect as the switch was thrown and lights flooded the inside of the house, Megan was nevertheless stunned by the sight that greeted her. Michael's beach house was just that: small and rumpled-looking, the furniture mismatched and chosen for comfort, not style.

"I warned you," he said, and smiled wryly as he spotted some dirty clothes flung into a corner chair.

"I thought you lived at the hotel."

"I have rooms there," he explained. "But I *live* here. I cook when I feel hungry—" he hooked a thumb toward a tiny kitchenette "—I clean up when I run out of room to stack things—" the gesture was expanded to include the clutter in the living area "—and I tell the world to go to hell in a fruit basket whenever the urge overtakes me."

This last was said as he steered Megan through the sitting room and out onto a wide wooden deck at the back of the house. Again her breath caught unexpectedly in her throat. Michael's beach house commanded a spectacular view of a moon-washed lagoon, the surface of the water so still and glasslike, it acted like a mirror for the millions of stars overhead. Farther out, the lagoon opened to the ocean, a vast, glittering stretch of water that disappeared over the horizon.

"It's so . . . beautiful," she whispered.

"I'm glad you like it. I do most of my hardest thinking out here on nights like this," he added. He moved up behind her and wrapped his arms around her waist. "The stars oblige me with nightly light shows, the dolphins swim right into the lagoon to keep me company. Best of all—" his lips pressed into the bare curve of her shoulder "—there isn't a neighbor for half a mile on either side, so I can kick off everything, not just my shoes, when I need to relax."

Megan's eyes fluttered shut. His fingers were busy at the nape of her neck, plucking out the pins that bound her hair and flinging them aside. When he was finished, he combed out the long, golden mass, spreading it across her shoulders, smoothing it against the satiny warmth of her skin.

"Your cousin was right, you know—you should let your hair down more often. It was one of the things that drove me crazy all those years ago. I used to lie awake at night wondering what your hair would feel like, what it would look like spread across a pillow."

Megan shuddered and gripped the top of the wooden railing more securely. His lips had not relented in their assault on the tender flesh of her neck, and his hands had roved to more compelling temptations. They lowered one strap, then the other, removing what flimsy support the plaited straps of fabric afforded the top of her dress.

"You're trembling," he murmured, chasing each strap down to her elbow.

"I'm frightened half out of my mind," she admitted with painful honesty. "It's been a long time for me, Michael. I'm not sure I remember the right things to do or say."

He was still for a long moment, then, "You don't have to say anything, if you don't want to. As for the right and wrong things to do, why don't you just leave those decisions up to me . . . unless, of course, you have some objections to the way I have handled them so far?"

"I have no objections at all," she said on a rushed breath.

"A sensible woman," he mused approvingly, his lips descending to work more of their magic.

"Oh, Michael—" Megan turned within the circle of his arms, her eyes raised searchingly to his "—that's exactly what I don't want to be tonight," she whispered fiercely. "I don't want to be sensible."

"You don't have to be anything you don't want to be," he insisted. "Not when you're here. Not when you're with me."

Moonlight sparkled off the brightness welling along her lashes and Michael's hands betrayed the stronger tremor that shook his body. His lips captured hers, their mouths slanting hungrily together, tongues and breaths mingling. His fingers threaded into the silken mane of her hair, caressing it with a reverence that brought a groan to his throat.

Sighs and whispers were exchanged as the heat within them grew to explosive torment. Tearing at the barriers of clothing between them, their bodies alternately strained apart and pressed together, hands, lips, tongues eager to explore havens of nakedness the instant they were freed.

Megan kicked away the last filmy shred of her clothing even as Michael was lifting her and carrying her inside to the bedroom. His body was hot and hard, a taut pillar of muscle sculpted into bands of sensual steel. His stride was powerful, yet graceful, urgent, yet measured to prolong the pleasure and the agony of anticipation. When he lowered her onto the bed, he knelt over her for a long, lingering moment, his raw male beauty stripping Megan of any shreds of doubt or hesitation that remained.

She opened her arms and reached up to him, a ragged cry welcoming the heat of his flesh alongside her own. His lips were there to taste the sound of his name, his hands to sweeten her cries, stroke by shivering stroke, into deep, shuddering sighs.

Megan's head thrashed from side to side on the pillow, the golden web of her hair loose and wild, causing Michael's heart to thunder. He rained a path of hot caresses from the curve of her shoulder to the ruched peaks of her breasts with his mouth. Over and over he rolled her nipple between his teeth and tongue, suckling her sweet flesh into the warmth and wetness of his mouth.

His thighs edged between hers and Megan rose to meet his flesh eagerly, joyously, shivering her way through a heartfelt groan of disbelieving wonder as she felt his strength and passion fill her.

Michael cried out in fierce pleasure the instant her body closed around him. His head arched back and his arms went rigid. The muscles across his chest and shoulders bunched with the incredible tension that began to build in his body—tension that threatened to undermine his few remaining threads of control. Megan's broken gasps were no help. Her supple, moist body offered no sympathy for his faltering sanity as each powerful thrust was drawn deeper and deeper into its tightening grip.

Once, twice, she stiffened and cried out beneath him and Michael's hands slid to her hips, levering her higher, bracing her as he sought the source of those shivering pulsations and demanded even more.

Megan, who would not have believed there could be more, felt a white-hot passion surge and swell within her. It rushed through her veins and flooded her soul. It seared her nerve endings in a tide of erupting ecstasy. She called out to Michael, reached out to him, clung to him as she felt his passion swell and shatter within him.

Megan's wild elation melted gradually into undulating languor. Her eyes quivered open and she stared unseeing at the patterns of moonlight dancing on the ceiling. Michael had collapsed into her arms, his body wonderfully damp and heavy. His breath panted lightly against her throat and instinctively she knew that he, too, had never before experienced anything quite so consuming or explosive. An unbidden rush of pride tested her restraint almost as much as the gentle, throbbing presence of his body where it still nestled deep within her, and she wanted to move against that hardness again. She wanted to remain locked in his arms and never let go. She wanted to laugh, to cry, to shout her joy out loud....

Michael stirred and propped his weight on his elbows. The light from the moon was barely bright enough to distinguish shape from shadow, and Megan wished she could see his face, his eyes, to know what he was thinking.

"You're frowning," he murmured. "Did I disappoint you?"

"Rather vain of you to ask, isn't it?" But she could hear the gentle sarcasm in his voice and she sensed the curving smile that accompanied it. "Especially when you already know the answer."

He lowered his mouth to hers, kissing her with enough confirmation to set her flesh tingling again.

"It wasn't vanity, I assure you," he said softly. "More like fear...or awe. In case I didn't say it clearly enough back at George's, you are one beautiful woman. The one who got away. The one I never dreamed would let me touch a hair on her head, never mind..." His voice faltered, as if he was searching for the right words and could not find them.

"Now who is accusing who of being vain," she protested weakly. She was close to tears for reasons she could not begin to fathom, closer still to acknowledging an emotion she had thought lost to her years ago.

"You were never vain," he objected. "Just overly cautious . . . then and now."

"One night after meeting you again, I end up in your bed, and you call that being cautious?"

His lips brushed over hers and his body shifted slightly. "What would you call it?" he asked in a whisper.

Megan heard the question, might even have been able to answer it if not for the fact that the subtle motion of his hips was commanding all her attention. He waited until her soundless gasp acquitted him of any charge of overeagerness before he sent his lips chasing after the rapidly fluttering pulse beat in her throat.

"For my own part," he mused, "I call it fulfilling a fantasy I have carried around with me for fifteen years, and if you wish to object, Counselor, you have about two seconds before I fulfill another."

"A-another?"

By way of a reply, his hands, mouth and body slid lower on the bed. The heated flickering insistence of his tongue demanded and won the sensual attentiveness of her breasts, then roved greedily downward to challenge the reflexive tension in her belly and thighs.

"Oh . . . ! No . . . !"

"Too late," he murmured, his mouth already plundering the soft and silken bounty.

Megan blushed from the tip of her toes to the roots of her scalp. She tried to remain calm and rational, knowing it was foolish to be feeling pangs of modesty, and yet, she was thirty-two years old, and she had never . . . No man had ever . . .

"Dear God," she gasped, and her hands twisted themselves into the folds of the sheets. "Michael...!"

But he was not listening. And after a few more moments, it did not matter anyway, for she was no longer crying out for him to stop, but pleading for him to continue.

8

MEGAN WAKENED SLOWLY, her senses responding grudgingly to the clean, crisp scent of sea air. A crescent of eyelashes was raised to verify the sunlight pouring through the open window; a muffled groan sealed them shut again as she turned her head and nestled it into the softness of the pillow.

She was alone in the rumpled bed. Vaguely, she remembered feeling the mattress bounce as Michael had departed some time ago, but she had fallen instantly back into a deep, exhausted sleep that Michael apparently thought deserved to go unbroken. And no wonder. Apart from catnaps during the night, neither one of them had been content to let the hours pass uneventfully. A sigh, a hand straying here or there, a leg shifting, or a word whispered in the most innocent of endearments was enough to trigger a response. She suspected Michael had indeed lived out his every fantasy—even one or two he had not thought of before last night.

A smile accompanied the now-familiar blush that seeped up her throat and shaded her face. She had always prided herself on being so conservative and reserved, always so perfectly in control of herself and her emotions. Last night had irrevocably shattered any and all illusions she may have had about her righteous self-discipline. Michael had made love to her freely and without inhibitions, and she had not only responded in kind, but had done so eagerly, spontaneously. She felt satiated. She felt radiant and glowing and fully alive for the first time in more years than she could remember.

Last night Michael had asked her about her marriage to Craig Thomas, and she had been nakedly honest. Craig had come along at a time in her life when she had been under the greatest pressure to comply with her family's expectations. She had given up a job in the public defender's office—a job she had truly loved— and joined the family law firm.

"You have to think about your future, Megan," her father had said sternly—and when had he ever spoken any other way? "You have to consider how best to achieve the goals you have set for yourself in life."

Goals *she* had set?

Craig Thomas had arrived on the scene then—brash and arrogant and handsome. The Thomases were wealthy and politically respected. Marrying Craig could only help to further her career ambitions.

Divorcing him should have had the opposite effect. But when the stories of his philandering and his chemical dependency were revealed, they added public sympathy to Megan's already high profile, and, three years later, she was offered the job as assistant district attorney under Philip Levy.

Her marriage had lasted less than two years. In all that time, Megan could not remember a single night when her husband's lovemaking had roused in her anything other than a feverish urgency to have it over and done. He had been a boorish and selfish lover. His need to prove his own prowess had overshadowed any desire for tenderness or shared pleasure.

Michael was just the opposite. He played her body like a finely tuned instrument, taking as much pleasure from orchestrating the various chords and crescendos of her ecstasy as achieving his own. Not one inch of her flesh had been considered too remote or too insignificant to have earned his full attention. Not one sense or sensation had been left unaffected. And in turn, she had reveled in exploring the mysteries of his body, mysteries that deepened her smile and heightened her flush with each recollection.

Megan stretched and rolled over onto her back. Where there had been patterns of moonlight during the night, there were now shredded streaks of sunlight dappling the ceiling. What would her family and friends think if they could see her now? Staid, stoic and stiffly upper-lipped, they undoubtedly would be shocked and outraged to see her sprawled naked in the glaring sunlight, her body aching gloriously from the attentions of a man . . . a man she should have been doing her utmost to pin down in a courtroom, not a bedroom.

Megan's smile faded.

As hard as she tried to force the ugly thoughts from her mind, the suspicions crept back to taunt her.

Michael was living in the Bahamas under his mother's maiden name—why? Because it was more glamorous, as he suggested, or because he knew it could not be easily traced?

Michael was a focal point of a justice department investigation. Did he manage the casino and resort as he claimed, or did he run a money-laundering operation for the syndicate? Either way, how had he come to have such power? And who were those men who had taken him to a business meeting at gunpoint? What kind of business would Colombians be interested in?

Megan pressed her hands to her temples, trying in vain to stop the barrage of questions—and conclusions. A glint of gold around her wrist caught her attention, and, with a gasp of bitter anguish, she tore it off and flung it at the wall opposite the bed.

"Whoa there," Michael cried, jerking back abruptly as the bracelet ricocheted off the wall and missed his cheek by an inch. "I hope it isn't anything I've said or done."

"Michael!"

He arched an eyebrow as he retrieved the bracelet. "You were expecting someone else?"

"No. No—of course not," she stammered. "It's just that I...I woke up and you weren't here, and...and..."

"And you missed me?" He smiled and his eyes roved meaningfully down the length of her body. "Then it appears I've returned from my morning swim just in time."

The heavy black waves of his hair were wet, his skin was damp and gleaming like newly polished teak. He dropped the towel he had draped loosely around his waist and came closer to the bed, but instead of joining her on it, which she more than half wanted him to do, he passed by and walked to a closet. He searched for a moment and found a pair of running shorts and a

T-shirt, which he tossed to Megan with a flip of his wrist.

"These should do. For my own part, the outfit you are wearing right now suits me just fine, but a few of the older residents on the bay might drill their binoculars straight back into their eye sockets if they saw you sailing past in your birthday suit."

"Sailing?" She caught the garments and held them in midair as she watched him cover his own nakedness with a pair of frayed denim cutoffs.

"Call it a picnic brunch, if you like. Or, you can call me a lazy bastard who doesn't own a pot or a pan. Either way—" he bent down and kissed her on the tip of her nose "—I know this secluded little place where black ties and evening gowns are definitely *not* de rigueur."

He kissed her again, this time on the forehead. "You've just got time for a quick shower before you're needed on deck."

"Aye aye, Captain. Your wish is my command."

He paused on his way back out the door and glanced over at the bed. He said nothing for a long moment, choosing to let her interpret his thoughts through his eyes—eyes that were a clearer, warmer shade of blue than she had ever seen before.

"Careful," he warned softly. "I could get to like the sound of that."

Then he was gone, and Megan was able to release the breath she had been unaware of holding. What had she seen in his eyes? A flicker of emotion that had made her chest constrict and her heart stumble over several erratic beats. Beautiful, he had called her last night. The one who had gotten away. Had he just been fulfilling a fantasy, or was it possible he was feeling the same emotional upheaval that had prompted Megan to reach out to him time and time again during the night?

What was it *she* was feeling? What did he make her feel? Alive, certainly, and more desirable than she had felt in years. Near the end of her marriage, the mere sight of her husband's naked body had repulsed her, the rough touch of his hands had turned her to ice. Moreover, in the eight years since their divorce, there hadn't been a man whose simple handshake had not elicited the same reaction, and she had begun to fear her heart had indeed turned to ice.

Michael had proven it hadn't—but at what cost? In those same eight years, Megan had gotten along quite nicely on her own strength. She had immersed herself in her profession with a single-mindedness that had relegated any and all personal concerns to the distant background. She hadn't wanted to be burdened by anymore emotional albatrosses, hadn't needed them. She certainly did not want or need them now, not if it meant suffering the tight, gripping ache that assailed her at the mere scent of Michael's flesh on the sheets beside her.

She had become strong and independent, conscientious and hardworking. She was more than qualified to step into Phil Levy's shoes when he retired, a prospect which brought tears of pride to her father's eyes when he considered it. She didn't need a Michael Vallaincourt in her life right now. She didn't need the complication, the temptation—not now, not ever!

Megan headed into the bathroom. She stepped into the shower stall and turned the water on full force, tilting her face into the needlelike spray until she could no longer distinguish the sting of tears from the rush of water.

It was no good. She had to tell Michael why she was in Freeport, and what she had been asked to do. What his reaction would be, she had no way of knowing. Anger, surely, for deceiving him. Disdain. Perhaps even hatred.

But it could only be worse if she said nothing, if she went sailing with him as if nothing was wrong, or if she let him make love to her again, or even let him touch her in that way that made her limbs melt and her heart leap within her chest . . .

Megan gasped and whirled around, blinking the water out of her eyes.

"I thought about where you were and what you were doing," Michael said as he stepped naked into the shower stall. "And I realized what a poor host I would be for not offering to scrub your back."

He moved closer and his hands brushed aside the sleek, wet curtain of her hair where it clung to her breasts. His palms engulfed her flesh, his fingers dancing lightly over the water-slicked surface of her skin. Before she could even think to open her mouth to protest, he was reaching for the bar of soap.

"Besides," he added as he lathered his hands, "I suddenly remembered another one of my fantasies."

"Michael, I—"

"Tut-tut. This is *my* fantasy. Turn around and behave."

His firm hands steered her around so that she was faced away from him. Using long, slow strokes, he spread the soap over her shoulders and back, massaging it down the length of her spine. There, he took deliberate care with the shapely curves of her hips and thighs, running his hands in patterns that made her curl her lower lip between her teeth and bite down sharply to keep from crying out.

The water streamed over them, filling the stall with heat and steam, the runoff swirling in foam-capped eddies around their feet.

Lovingly, Michael's hands prowled beneath her outstretched arms and circled lasciviously around her breasts. The velvety-soft nipples earned an extra leisurely concentration of delicious torment until they were hard as berries and etching their need into the palms of his hands.

Megan's breath began to come in shallow pants. She leaned back against him and reached up to send her fingers combing into his hair. His erection was pushing against her, rising hard and determined and she returned the provocation by rolling gently, rhythmically into his heat.

He accepted the challenge with a husky laugh and, replenishing his hands with more soap, sent his questing fingers lower, smoothing them over her belly and hips, kneading thick white peaks in the nest of yellow curls. His fingers delved and stroked, introducing all manner of sleek, wild sensations to flesh that quivered and pressed greedily into his ministrations. Megan's entire body quaked with the pleasure. She turned her head and tried to capture his mouth, but her own wracking shudders prevented her from doing more than blinding him with the smeared veil of her hair.

Aroused beyond comprehension, Megan let herself be turned and crowded back against the water-splashed tiles. His soapy hands cradled her neck and he kissed her, his tongue ravishing her mouth the way his fingers had ravished her flesh. The water rained down on them, sheeting off their bodies as Michael lifted her and brought them lustfully together. Megan wrapped her legs eagerly around his waist, already moving urgently against him, moving into him before he was fully braced or even prepared for the drenching onslaught of pleasure.

The soap had made her slick enough that he groaned with the silky friction, driving deeply, aggressively into her until his own shuddering ecstasy was only a threat away. He felt the heat showering through him and over him and he threw his head back, gripping her tighter as their combined need to move faster, thrust deeper nearly undermined his ability to ride out the shattering torrents of sensation.

Only when the last shiver had been gasped free, and the last ripple of tension had been shocked from their bodies did Michael gradually ease his grip, lowering Megan so that she could share the burden of support. He continued to hold her, continued to caress her with his body and consume her with his mouth until he became aware of the water turning cool on his back and shoulders.

Tottering out of the stall on unsteady limbs, Megan stood meekly by while he bundled her in a warm towel and rubbed her dry.

When it was her turn to reciprocate, she lingered so long over the lean, hard contours of his body, that if not for the sharp, unexpected *bonggg* of the door chimes, she might have been tempted to linger even longer.

"That will be brunch," Michael murmured, his hand brushing tenderly over her cheek. "But promise me you'll hold that thought for later."

He left the bathroom, the towel wrapped around his waist. Megan watched him go, and when his path took him across her own pale reflection in the partly misted mirror, she was shocked by the sight of the stranger who stared back at her. Her eyes seemed inordinately large and dark, the centers dilated with the effects of her spent passion. Her mouth looked sinfully debauched, and her body...

Megan closed her eyes and sighed. She hadn't told him. She hadn't resisted him. She hadn't even had the strength or compunction to worry that the soap dish had left its imprint on her hip.

Smiling, shaking her head ruefully, Megan dressed and emerged from the bathroom in time to see Michael exchanging some bills for a huge wicker picnic hamper. The delivery boy gaped at the tip in his hand and grinned.

"Thanks, Mr. Vallaincourt! Have a nice day."

"We intend to."

"HOW CAN YOU get along with no food in the house?" she asked a short while later as she balanced her weight against the rocking motion of Michael's sailboat.

"I didn't say I didn't have *any* food in the house," Michael corrected her. "I just thought we might need something more substantial than beer and pretzels."

Megan relaxed and watched him expertly maneuver the small craft through the narrow mouth of his lagoon and out into open water. The sea was a startlingly clear turquoise blue, the sky a vast azure vault overhead. Michael's ruggedly handsome features were perfectly suited to such a breathtaking backdrop. Megan had no difficulty envisioning him with his black hair swept back in a piratical ponytail, his long legs braced against the roll and sway of a massive wooden deck, a jewel winking in his ear and a sword flashing in his hand.

The sleek white sailboat skimmed gracefully over the waves and in no time at all, Michael was tacking toward the shallower water surrounding a tiny islet. The cay was no more than a hundred paces across at its widest point—an oasis of pale pink sand and stately palms in the middle of the bright blue sea.

It was a wonderful place for a picnic, and once again Megan found it easy to forget the rest of the world even existed. They brunched on baskets of cold shrimp and calamari salad, freshly baked croissants, fruit and cheese. Two bottles of chilled wine had been packed into the hamper, one of which they drank as they ate, the other Michael anchored in the water to keep cool.

When there was nothing left but crumbs and soiled cutlery, Michael stretched out in the shade of a palm tree, his back propped against the trunk, his eyes closed against the lulling combination of surf and gentle sea breezes. He lit one of his aromatic cigars and looked very much like a man without a care in the world.

Megan could not resist reaching over and combing her fingers through the dark, thick waves of his hair. He smiled and, with his eyes still closed, circled an arm around her shoulders and drew her down beside him. His skin was warm beneath her cheek and the sound of his heart beating only inches away was an intoxicant far more potent than the wine they had consumed. Her fingers traced tiny whorls through the forest of hairs on his chest, and her eyelids grew contentedly heavy. A sigh found its way to her lips and she snuggled even closer, smiling her own secret smile as she relaxed against the rhythm of his hand stroking the nape of her neck.

"I have this very strong urge to cut the anchor and let the boat drift away," he remarked pensively.

"Sounds wonderful. How long would it take for someone to find us?" she asked, raising her head for a moment.

"Oh . . . about an hour." He laughed and pointed to the leisure boats that were chasing the wind along the coast of the big island.

"Too bad," Meg mused, nestling back down into the cradle of his body. "I think I could get used to this."

His fingers paused in their sensual massage and, after a few moments of thoughtful silence, he slipped his hand beneath her chin and tilted her face up to his.

"Could you really?"

"Could I really what?" she asked dreamily.

"Could you really give it all up? The big clients, the big office, and the big, shiny letters beneath your name? Could you really dare disappoint your family and friends by not living up to their every expectation?"

Megan studied his expression, stunned by the questions, and even more stunned by the seriousness prompting them.

"Could you?" she countered softly.

"You seem to have forgotten—my greatest ambition in life was to tour the country on my Harley and set myself up with a rich widow."

Megan's eyes narrowed. "No. As I recall, you were quite adamant about touring the country on your Harley, but only because you didn't want to be tied down to any one place or any one person."

"Funny how things change when you grow older," he said.

"Isn't it though. You do seem pretty well tied up to the Privateer's Paradise."

Michael grinned slowly. "You might be surprised to know how quickly I could walk away from it all."

"The casino? The Ferrari? The beautiful women, the action, the excitement?" The danger, she almost added. And the obligations to whoever or whatever had brought him to the Bahamas.

"Managing the casino is just a job, and the Ferrari is nice, but it's just a car. The action? The excitement? Drunk tourists and cardsharps who try to cheat the house are not exactly my idea of stimulating challenges."

"So why do you stay?"

The gleam in his eyes that had been commanding all her attention vanished as quickly as it had appeared and he grinned slyly. "Because of the beautiful women, of course."

"Of course," she murmured.

"But I will admit, it is a tempting thought just to give it all the heave-ho—the headaches, the aggravations, the frustrations. Give it all up and settle down on some deserted island, a good woman by my side, the earth for a bed, the stars for a blanket. Sound appealing?"

"What would you live on?" she asked, eyeing the expensive picnic hamper. "Raw fish and coconuts?"

Michael followed her gaze and chuckled. "For as long as I could, I guess, and then I'd have to look for that rich widow to support my bad habits. Or maybe a rich divorcée," he added and claimed her lips beneath his own. When she was well and thoroughly kissed, he eased his grip slightly and stared at her flushed, dewy features.

"I'm having another larcenous thought," he warned silkily.

"Another?"

"Mmm. Kidnapping is still a felony, is it not?"

"There were . . . mitigating circumstances," she answered, her voice stumbling over a breath as she felt his hand slide up beneath her T-shirt.

"What if I compound the crime?"

Her lips trembled visibly as his fingers stroked suggestively around the raised nub of her nipple. "Compound it . . . how?"

"By holding you hostage a few more days. There are a few jobs I'd like to take care of around the beach house. You could help me, or you could just play bare-foot in the sand and watch."

"We couldn't. *I* couldn't!"

"Why not?" he demanded. "You said yourself you had no hard-and-fast schedule to stick to."

"Yes, I know, but..."

"But what?"

Megan turned her head slightly and looked away from the probing blue eyes. "Shari would think I had lost my mind completely."

Michael stared at the top of her head, watching the play of sunlight on the tousled, windswept tangle of her ponytail. Long, blond tendrils trailed down her neck and over her shoulders, and he suffered pleasurably through a vivid recollection of the heavy, wet silk of it clinging to his skin in the shower.

She wasn't the only one who was in danger of losing touch with reality. Fifteen years had vanished in the blink of an eye and it was as if they had never been apart, never traveled separate roads, never shared half a lifetime of memories with other people.

A surge of the old rebellion made him press her down onto the sand beside him.

"I want you to spend the next few days with me. Will you do it?"

"The next few days? But I...I can't just leave Shari on her own."

"Shari looks like a girl who can handle herself. Be-sides, she won't be on her own. I have a feeling Gino will be only too happy to look out for her."

"But...my clothes, my...my things..."

"My promise," he murmured, sliding his hand down to where her T-shirt was knotted at her waist, "is to keep you warm and covered every minute of every hour of every day until you're too weak to stand, never mind worry about clothes."

Megan's eyes widened as she felt his mouth close hungrily over the bead of her nipple. Threading her fingers into his hair, she succumbed to the tremors his tongue invoked, her heart throbbing with joy, her conscience sighing with the helplessness of it all.

9

MEGAN WOULD NOT have been surprised to discover the key to bungalow four no longer fit. She had been gone three days, but it felt like three years, and she fully expected to find the rooms empty, her baggage growing cobwebs in the lost and found.

She was dressed, as she had been for the past three days, in an assortment of Michael's clothes: a cotton shirt was tied in a knot at her midriff, topping a pair of gray running shorts. the dress she had worn to the party—the dress that had cost her a month's wages—was crumpled at the bottom of a plastic grocery bag and slung over her shoulder. Her hair was haphazardly clipped in a knot on the top of her head, with more trailing out than in. She wore no makeup, carried her shoes in her hand and had smiled and bade a happy good evening to several strolling couples she had passed on her way through the hotel grounds.

Opening the door of the bungalow, she tossed the plastic bag and her shoes into the nearest corner and flicked on the light switch. She heard a startled gasp and saw first one, then another disheveled head rise above the back of the sofa.

"Meg!" Shari said, blinking owlishly in the sudden glare of light. "You're back!"

Megan looked amusedly from Shari's flushed face to the more robust, Mediterranean features of Gino Romani. His shirt was flung on the floor beside them, his trousers were loose and wriggled halfway down his hips. Shari was in no better condition and it was embarrassingly clear to Megan that she had interrupted them at a most inopportune time.

"I . . . um . . . could go out and come back again in a few minutes," Megan offered, unsuccessfully concealing a smile.

"Well, I . . ." Shari's face was turned away as she fumbled to rearrange her clothing.

"No problem," said Megan. "Take your time, I'll just be outside by the pool."

Still smiling, she walked back along the white gravel pathway and settled into an empty lounge chair. With the sun fully set, there were few people left outdoors; most were dining or turning their sights more eagerly to the casino tables.

Megan lay back and drank in the fragrant air. She could still taste Michael on her lips, feel him on her skin. If she closed her eyes, she could even feel him inside her, sleek and full, thrusting them both to tumultuous heights of oblivion.

The three days with Michael had been bliss. They had slept late each morning and breakfasted in the shade of the lagoon. They had walked for hours along the sun-drenched beach, their conversations relaxed and easy, their only arguments arising over what to eat and where to eat it. Megan had challenged him to live off the land, rather than the local delicatessen, and he had taken up the gauntlet by trapping lobster and crab and boiling them over an open fire. He had shinned up a palm tree and knocked down a dozen ripe coconuts, and, after cracking them open with a knife, had made them drinks with rum and the fresh, sweet milk.

They had sailed to the tiny cay each day and made love under the awning of palm trees. They had clung to each other in the lagoon, matching the slow, languorous rhythm of their bodies to the ebb and flow of the surf. At night, they had lain breathless and satiated in the blue-white glow of the moonlight, falling fast asleep in each other's arms, knowing they would awaken that way in the morning.

Michael hadn't accomplished many of his jobs. He had fixed a loose board on the deck and that was about it. He had also, like a small mischievous boy, taken her by the hand and led her to a locked shed behind the beach house. The Harley was kept there, a big black machine with enough chrome parts for three normal cars. He had taken Megan on a wild ride around the island, and when they had returned, their lovemaking had been just as wild and reckless and exhilarating.

Megan opened her eyes. The door to bungalow four had opened, sending a slash of white light out into the darkness. Gino stood in the glare while he tucked the bottom edge of his shirt into his trousers. The top of Shari's head barely reached the top of Gino's breastbone, and with effortless ease, he leaned forward and scooped her up in one arm, holding her for the duration of a kiss that left them both wide-eyed and smiling.

He stole one last quick kiss and, after a few hastily whispered words, he was gone, the crunch of his shoes carrying him hurriedly along the pathway toward the hotel.

Megan saw Shari searching the shadows, then take a deep breath and walk over to where Megan was sitting by the pool.

For a long moment, neither one said anything. Neither one dared meet the other's eye until one furtive glance led to another, and caused them both to surrender to a burst of laughter.

"A fine pair of chaperons we'd make," Shari managed finally. She plumped down on an adjacent lounge chair and stretched out with a delicious sigh. "God, I'm having a wonderful time. Whose idea was this anyway? Do we really have to go back home next week?"

"I take it you haven't missed me too much," Meg said dryly.

"I haven't missed you at all," Shari declared. "Oh Meg…Meg, he's wonderful! He's clumsy and cute and funny. He was so darned serious about being a gentleman and not giving me the wrong impression, it's taken me all this time just to get him in a room alone! And there we were, this close…well—" she giggled and lewdly amended the span between her hands "—this close to doing something about it, and who shows up?"

"Sorry," Megan said. "How was I supposed to know?"

"Never mind. He won't get away so easily." Shari sighed happily and collapsed against the cushions. Her smile broadened as she lifted an eyebrow in Megan's direction. "You don't exactly look as if you have been suffering these past few days."

"No," Megan admitted quietly. "I haven't."

Shari sat up and swung her legs over the side of the lounge. She peered closely at her cousin, noting the uncharacteristic disarray of her hair and clothing, the unbroken tan glowing healthily through the shadows. Even more telling was the clear, bright sparkle in the depths of the jade-green eyes. All traces of fatigue and strain were gone, replaced by a softness Shari hadn't seen in years.

"My God," she whispered. "You're in love."

"Don't be ridiculous," Megan answered, the denial a breath too slow in coming, and far too quiet to be convincing.

"I'm not. And you are! It's written all over your face! Does he know? Does he feel the same way? What are you going to do about it? Has he asked you to—"

"He hasn't asked me anything," Megan interrupted. "And before you work yourself up to a full head of steam, *Ms. Fairbreast*, he hasn't said anything, he doesn't know anything, and as far as I'm concerned, there is nothing for either of us to ask, know or say, so just let the subject drop!"

"But, Meg—"

"Look, can't we just enjoy the rest of our vacation without tacking on any more complications? I enjoy Michael's company. We have fun together and he makes me laugh. I'm relaxed. I'm falling madly in love with the palm trees and the pink sand, but that's it. That's all. When the two weeks are over, I'll go back to New York and Michael will get on with running his casino."

"You could do that? You could just fly away from him and get on with your life?"

"You say that as if I have a choice!"

"People always have choices. You could choose to get off the political carousel you're on before someone else takes the initiative and pushes you off. You could choose to go back to doing what you have always wanted to do—practice privately and on a small scale. The happiest I ever saw you was when you worked in that cramped little legal aid office, taking cases from people who didn't have two cents to rub together. You were happy, Meg, without the Yves St. Laurent suits and the Gucci shoes. You are a damned good lawyer and you don't need the sanction of your father or brothers to prove it. You have always done what *they* thought was best for you—why don't you do what *you* want to do for a change?"

"It isn't that easy."

"Why not? Thousands of people do it every day. If you listen real carefully, you can actually hear them laughing, having a good time. It isn't a sin, Meg. It isn't even a crime to want something *less* than what someone else wants for you."

Megan turned away, a retort burning in her throat. But what could she say—that Shari was wrong? She wasn't wrong, not entirely. Megan had loved her dusty, cluttered legal aid office, and she had loved the childishly scrawled notes and bottles of homemade wine that had come to her as payment for her services. Her family had humored her enthusiasm as long as they thought she was just paying her dues to gain experience and recognition. But when the invitation to join the district attorney's office had come, her father had ordered the champagne and hired the caterers before bothering to ask if she had accepted the position.

No, she wasn't happy as in bells and whistles and exploding fireworks, but she was content. It was still her own hard work that had gotten her to where she was in the department; she was resting on no one's laurels but her own. But was being *content* the best she could hope for? And was it enough?

What about Michael? He had made her laugh. He had been warm and tender and loving, and it was that side of him that had won her heart unquestioningly. But what about the other side, the darker side? He had promised to explain his behavior of the other night, but had not broached the subject again in their three days together, and she had not asked. It stood between them like a wall, as did the memory of the hard, angry frost in his eyes the morning she had confronted him on the patio. What had angered him the most—the accusation that he was involved in illegal activities, or the suspicion that she was not here on an innocent vacation? Either or both must certainly be playing on Michael's mind the same way her own suspicions and doubts kept cropping up to torment her.

Especially if he had something to hide.

In love with him? Yes, she was. Happily? Not by a long shot.

"Megan Worth, you haven't heard a word I've said," Shari groused.

"No. No, I guess I haven't."

"Well? What are you going to do?"

"Do?" Megan sighed. "First of all, I am going to go inside and indulge in a long, hot bath. Then I plan to curl up with a nice, boring book—like the *Traveler's*

Guide to Coping with Meddlesome Roommates—and sleep the rest of the night away."

Shari frowned and glanced over Megan's shoulder. "Are you sure you had no other plans?"

Megan followed Shari's gaze and felt a familiar tightening sensation in the pit of her belly as she recognized Michael's tuxedoed form walking toward them along the pathway. Like a chameleon, he had shed the carefree, restful guise of a beachcomber and changed it for the handsome, perfectly groomed elegance of a resort manager, and he had done it with a swiftness that left Megan a little unsteady in the knees.

Shari had perked up like a bloodhound, giving him the kind of speculative look that would have made any self-respecting bachelor run for cover.

"Miss Stevenson." He greeted Shari with a nod and a smile. "I hope I haven't spoiled your vacation by keeping Megan away for so long."

"You spoiled it by bringing her back," she said candidly. "Gino and I were just getting to . . . know each other better . . . if you catch my meaning."

Michael laughed softly. "I wondered why he blew past me a while ago like a scalded cat. For all his size and bluster, he's pretty shy around most women. You must have made quite an impression."

"I could say the same thing about someone else I know," Shari said pointedly. "Not that she would ever admit it, of course, but Meg was practically a recluse back home. I was just telling her what a shame I thought it was that we have to fly back next week. On the other hand, we don't *have* to rush back. I mean, Meg hasn't taken a vacation in years. I'm sure no one would object to her staying on an extra week or two. As for me, well, I'm my own boss, so if I want extra time off, who is going to argue with me?"

"Ah yes." Michael smiled and diplomatically ignored the savage pinch Megan gave Shari's upper arm. "Megan was telling me you write novels."

Shari moved a prudent step away and rubbed her arm. "Romance novels, actually. Quite good, I'm told, and very believable. If you're interested, Meg has a copy of my latest one, *Heart of Stone*. Being as sophisticated and cultured as she is, dear Meg turned her nose up at the plot line at first, but now she might just be ready to admit that the plot and characters are fascinatingly true to life. Well—" she looked from one amused face to the other livid one, then beamed at Michael "—I think it's time for me to take a stroll along the beach. If you two will excuse me . . ."

Michael and Megan watched Shari weave her way between the palm trees that led to the beach. Megan's cheeks were flaming and she was thankful for the cooling shadows. Michael seemed nonplussed by the blatant matchmaking, but she thought she saw him work the tip of a finger under his collar to ease its grip.

"I wonder if Gino knows he's a marked man," Michael mused.

"I'd be glad to give him some helpful tips."

"He's a big boy. He knows what he's doing."

"And I'm a big girl," she cried softly, "but I don't have a clue what I'm doing, Michael. I don't have a clue what either of us are doing, do you?"

Michael took her gently into his arms. The threat of panic was in her voice, too close to the surface to brush away with a joke, so he buried his lips in her hair and held her, and gave her the time she needed to get herself under control again.

"I know I promised you a quiet evening on your own," he said, as he tilted her chin upward. "But I took one look at the mountain of messages and mail waiting for me at the front desk and, well, I thought chateaubriand for two sounded much more appealing. I was hoping you might think so, too."

"Oh, Michael, I don't know..."

He bowed his head and kissed her, but what started out being a casual, reassuring caress, turned into something far more passionate and meaningful. When he lifted his mouth away from hers, he continued to gaze deeply into her eyes, and for the first time, his emotions were there for her to see, stark and unguarded.

"We have some things to talk about, Megan Worth. No, I don't know what we're doing, or where any of this will lead, but I do know you weren't out of my sight ten minutes and it nearly drove me crazy. There are some...things...you have to know about me. Some things I should have told you before and have to tell you now before they drive me crazy, too." He glanced at his watch and cursed softly under his breath. "I still have to check in at the casino, but that shouldn't take me too long. Here—" something cold and metallic was pressed into her hand "—this is the key to my suite. I've already ordered dinner. I'll meet you there in, say, an hour?"

"An hour," she whispered. "All right."

He kissed her again, then jammed his hands into his pockets as he backed away. "Ten minutes drove me crazy. In an hour, I should be ready for a padded cell. Don't be late."

Megan walked slowly back to the bungalow, her composure defeated again . . . this time by the unaccustomed sensation of tears.

It wasn't possible . . . was it? Michael couldn't be in love with her . . . could he?

Megan ran a steaming hot bath and tried to soak away some of her confusion, but with one vigilant eye trained on the clock, it was difficult to concentrate on anything other than the anticipation churning in her belly. Half of her allotted time was used up bathing and drying her hair, the other half was spent selecting just the right thing to wear.

A determined search of the bureau drawers brought forth an erotically skimpy camisole and matching satin panties. The minidress she chose was cut in a deep vee in front, and molded snugly enough to her figure to contrast any lingering memories of sloppy T-shirts and oversized jogging shorts. Not that she was deliberately setting out to influence him, or anything, but if there was a chance . . . the slightest chance . . .

Megan looked around sharply at the sound of a knock at the door. Shari had not yet returned from her stroll along the beach and Megan supposed she had forgotten to take her key.

"Another five minutes and you would have been out of luck," Megan began, the words dying in her throat as she opened the door and found herself staring up into the dark and shadowy features of the last person she expected to see.

10

"EVENIN' MA'AM. I hope I ain't disturbin' y'all."

It was Dallas.

The tall, white-haired Texan was silhouetted in the doorway, hat in hand, a sheepish grin on his face, and an approving twinkle in his eye as he pursed his lips and offered a faint whistle of appreciation.

"Whoo-ee, you look fitter than a filly at a fairground."

"I . . . er, was just getting dressed to go to dinner."

"Lucky feller, whoever he is. I won't keep y'all very long, but I was hopin' I could have a private word with you."

Frowning, Megan opened the door wider and invited him to step inside. Instinctively she glanced, as he did, out into the gloom ringing the bungalow before she closed the door behind him.

"I been tryin' to catch up to y'all for the past two, three days now," he said. "You been off seein' the sights?"

"I spent a few days . . . on the other side of the island," Megan explained. "Was there any particular reason you were looking for me?"

Dallas scratched thoughtfully at his chin and arched one of his bushy white eyebrows. "Well, as a matter of fact, I thought you was the one lookin' fer me."

"Looking for you? I don't understand. Did someone tell you I was looking for you?"

"Y'all told me yourself, gal." The smile hardly wavered, nor did the wing of his eyebrow descend in the slightest degree as he reached into the breast pocket of his jacket and withdrew a slim leather billfold. The badge identifying him as a treasury agent caught the overhead light and glittered dully off Megan's astonished eyes.

Dallas was the agent Hornsby had put in place in the resort. Dallas was the one who had been alerted to Megan's arrival in Freeport, and he was the one who was supposed to make contact when he saw her wearing the gold bracelet.

But she had only had the damned bracelet on for half a day, most of that spent on a secluded part of the beach! She hadn't seen Dallas anywhere near the water, or the restaurant . . .

"Y'all look like you got a bone stuck in your craw. You all right?"

"Yes. I'm fine. Just . . . fine." She remembered. Dallas had been one of the few people she had bumped into on her way to the party in the grand ballroom. A few minutes earlier, he would have been safely lost in the crowd of gamblers; a few minutes later, she would have been safely whisked away in Michael's arms.

"Maybe you'd like to tell me what it was you wanted to tell me, so's we can both jest get on with what we was doin'?"

Megan opened her mouth and closed it again without speaking.

"Funny thing, you know?" he said, his eyes narrowing speculatively. "That there Vallaincourt ain't been around the past few days, either. I asked his secretary casuallike where he was, and she told me he took a couple of days off to go fishin'. Imagine that. Fishin'."

Megan walked to the patio doors. The moon was not yet up over the horizon, but there were a million stars paving its way. Someone from the hotel had organized a party down on the beach, and a fire was blazing, throwing sparks up into the night sky.

"Now, it ain't any of my business how y'all go about renewin' an acquaintance with an old friend. It *is* my business if you know something about that old friend that might assist us in an investigation." Dallas's eyes were screwed down to slits. "Abner Hornsby told me you was a smart young filly—too smart to put a gaudy old trinket around your wrist by mistake, and too smart to forget the reason why you put it there. By rights, then, it also makes you too danged smart to forget why you was sent down here in the first place."

Megan closed her eyes, but that only made it worse, for Michael's face was all she could see, and Michael's voice was all she could hear.

We have some things to talk about. Things you have to know about me. Things I should have told you before...

One of the reasons she had not pressed Michael for too many details about his business dealings, and why she had not been able to work up the courage to tell him exactly why she was here was that she was frightened of having to hear her worst suspicions confirmed. If they were, if she discovered an unpleasant truth about

Michael Antonacci/Vallaincourt, she would have been
faced with the even more terrible dilemma of what to
do about it.

As a lawyer, she was bound by oath to report any and
all crimes and criminal activities. Loving the man suspected of those crimes did not exempt her from the role
of accessory if those crimes were corroborated. Nor
was a lover automatically a client, giving her the buf-
fer of attorney-client privilege to fall back on.

"I'd shor' hate to see a pretty little thing like you ru-
ined by one dumb mistake," Dallas said quietly.

Megan turned and met his gaze. It was odd, but she
hadn't noticed before that Dallas's wide-beamed face
and stocky build bore more than a faint similarity to her
father's lantern jaw and barrel chest. The grandfa-
therly air that had appealed to her the first night in the
casino had vanished along with the kindly crinkles at
the corners of his eyes. Dallas was the symbol of authority now. An authority Megan had been disci-
plined to respect long before she had ever attended law
school.

"Since neither one of us is gettin' any younger wait-
in' on you makin' up your mind about somethin' or
other," he said slowly, "maybe it would help move
things along a little if I tell you what we found out in
the three days you was off *visitin'*. Seems your friend has
been playin' his cards pretty close to his chest. Seems
he don't own this here fancy cow palace a'tall. Seems
he just runs it, like he's been runnin' a lot o' things over
the past ten years or so...for his boss...Vincent
Giancarlo."

11

MEGAN THOUGHT she knew how a condemned man felt as he was being led to the gallows. Her heart was pounding in her throat, lodged there by a lump of guilt so thick she could not swallow it free no matter how hard she tried. Her hands were cold and clammy. Her skin was a sheath of ice. Her footsteps were slow and wooden, and seemed mired in a nightmare in which the rest of the world sped by around her, but where she managed to get nowhere fast.

Michael's suite of rooms were on the top floor. Waiting for the elevator took a small eternity; watching guests who stepped in behind her and pushed the buttons to light up every floor between one and fifteen made her clench her teeth so hard her gums ached.

The key was brass, designed to look like an old-fashioned passkey for a treasure chest. Megan clutched it in her hand as she knocked on the door; she was well over the hour time limit and hoped Michael would already be there waiting.

But he wasn't. The rooms were romantically backlit and there were fresh cut flowers in a large vase on the coffee table. An ice bucket cradled a chilling bottle of champagne, and a table had been set up on the balcony for their dinner. The unlit candles were waiting, the starlight was primed. There were six huge rooms and two bathrooms, all furnished for a segment of *Lifestyles of the Rich and Famous*, but Megan saw none of it. She searched the suite and paced away nearly half an hour more before deciding to look for him elsewhere.

She took the elevator back down to the lobby and went into the casino, the first logical place to begin her search. A quick scan of the room was unsuccessful. The rows of slot machines were full, the tables congested; she recognized one or two faces from the restaurant and the beach, but Michael's dark hair and broad shoulders were nowhere in sight.

"Excuse me," she said, approaching one of the tuxedoed security guards. "Have you seen Mr. Vallaincourt recently?"

An appreciative eye took in the shortness of her dress as well as the curves it flattered.

"I believe he was here a while ago, but..." He shrugged apologetically and smiled. "You might try his office."

Megan thanked him and retraced her steps to the lobby. Several limousines were in the process of emptying their passengers, and the foyer was crowded and noisy; Megan hurriedly bypassed the reception area and walked toward the row of offices behind the lobby. There were three large oak doors, banded in brass, bearing the names and positions of persons in authority. With a mixed sense of dread and resignation, Megan approached the one marked Manager.

There was no immediate response to her knock.

She glanced over her shoulder, but the newly arrived tourists were five deep at the reception desk. She

tried the doorknob and was surprised to feel it turn
easily. The door swung open on well-oiled hinges and
Megan first peeked, then stepped inside what was obviously a secretary's outer office. After a second, pre-
cautionary glance out at the lobby, she went all the way
in and closed the door behind her.

An arrangement of cozy rattan furniture occupied
one corner of the office; a large, neatly organized desk
guarded the approach to the second set of wide floor-
to-ceiling double oak doors. One of them was ajar by
several inches, open wide enough to allow Megan to see
Michael standing behind his desk.

She took a couple of eager steps forward, then halted
again, her heart once more rising to press at the base of
her throat.

Lit only by a pair of green banker's lamps, Michael's
rugged handsomeness overwhelmed her. Why? Why
did he have to look so charming and devil-may-care?
Why hadn't he aged and grown fat and pockmarked
with dissipation? He didn't look like a gangster, for
heaven's sake. He didn't look at all—if Dallas's report
was to be believed—like Vincent Giancarlo's most
trusted right-hand man.

The burly Texan had practically crowed with delight
when she had given him Michael's real name—*betrayed* his real name. But what other choice did she
have? She had worn the damned bracelet in a fit of anger and it had been just her luck that Dallas had seen it
during those brief five minutes in the lobby. Lying to
him about it, or about Michael, would not have saved
either one of them grief. The best she could hope for
now was that Michael would understand why she had

done what she had done and not hate her too much. That he'd give her the chance to unravel this mess . . . if it wasn't too late already.

Michael frowned as he bent over his desk, but it only gave his chiseled ruggedness a sharper, cleaner edge. It also drew her attention, however reluctantly, to the squareness of his jaw, the sensual fullness of his mouth, the long-lashed seductiveness of his eyes. An image of their naked bodies twined together, gleaming faintly by candlelight, undulating sinuously by moonlight, threatened to defeat Megan before she had even begun, and she knew she had to proceed quickly, without thinking, without delaying to wonder what could have been, what might have been under different circumstances.

Not bothering to knock or otherwise announce her presence, Megan pushed the doors wide open and walked boldly into Michael's office.

He looked up sharply, the frown on his face giving way to shock. "Megan—?"

"Michael, I have to see you. I have to talk to you, if only for a few minutes. There is something important you have to know."

"Megan, I—"

"No. Please, let me speak. Let me get this out before I lose my nerve completely and then you can kick me out, or do whatever it is you want to do with me."

"*Megan!* I'd like nothing better than to talk to you, but, *as you can see* I'm a little tied up at the moment."

Megan followed his glance, and the words, the breath, the ability to think or move ground to a dead halt. Michael was not alone. Seated on the sofa in a dimly lit corner of the room was the short, swarthy Colombian she had seen in the casino; beside him, looking as coolly ominous as he had in a courtroom eighteen months ago, was Vincent Giancarlo.

Flanking both men were identically grim bodyguards, and, opposite them, wearing an expression as studiously blank as Michael's was Gino Romani.

Megan could only stare, aghast, as Vincent Giancarlo rose to his feet. It seemed to take a long time, and when he was completely upright, he gave the impression of filling the entire room. It was only an impression, of course, for he was several inches shorter than Michael, and not nearly so formidably muscular in build. Giancarlo was impeccably groomed, however, not a dark brown hair out of place or a smudge of dulling grime on his snakeskin shoes. His eyes, dark and deep-set, gave Megan the feeling he could see right through her and if her feet had not suddenly become rooted to the floor, she would have turned and fled without a second thought.

"Michael—" he had a low, throaty voice, as smooth as silk and just as seductive "—you've been keeping secrets from me, I see."

Megan saw the tension shiver along Michael's jaw before he managed a wan smile. "Mrs. Thomas and I are old friends—we went to school together. She's vacationing on the islands for a couple of weeks."

Giancarlo walked over to where Megan stood. "Everyone should have such lovely old friends. And I can see now why a man who has not taken so much as an afternoon off work in over a year suddenly plays hooky for three days." The large, liquid-brown eyes turned to Michael. "I approve."

"I . . . I'm sorry," Megan stammered. "I didn't mean to interrupt you."

"Nonsense." Giancarlo took a firm grip on her hand. "Such interruptions are what keep a man's blood flowing. It is you who must excuse us. Obviously, you had plans together for this evening, and it is we who are interrupting you."

Megan suppressed a shiver as he permitted himself a deliberately suggestive appraisal of her appearance. The dress she wore was suddenly far too short, too tight, and definitely too revealing for comfort, and she inwardly cursed her frivolous urge in selecting it.

"Really," she said breathlessly, "it was nothing important. We were just going to have dinner."

"Just dinner?" Giancarlo's mellow accent caressed the words. "Mrs. Thomas, may I say if my wife ever dressed like this 'just for dinner' I would have a dozen strapping sons by now and be twenty pounds thinner. Michael—you should have told us."

"You should have told me you were coming, Vince," Michael countered evenly.

"Ah, touché. Unfortunately, however, I didn't know myself until a few hours ago. And besides, I prefer to come and go unexpectedly. It keeps everyone on their toes . . . don't you agree, Eduardo?"

The dark little Colombian had been doing his best to remain as unobtrusive as possible. At the mention of his name, he shifted uncomfortably in his seat and nodded, which earned a hearty laugh from the Sicilian. "Then again, some men never like surprises. Not even the luscious ones. Michael, you mustn't let us interfere with your plans. I would never forgive myself if I was the cause of such a lovely lady going hungry for the sake of a boring business meeting. Furthermore—" he glanced at his Rolex and scowled "—if I'm not mistaken, the last time I ate something was when the sun was coming up this morning. Is that crazy Alsatian chef still working here? The one who melts a pound of butter with a pound of cheese and makes it into a pasta sauce?"

"René," Michael said. "He's still here."

"Then it's settled. Eduardo and I will test René's culinary skills and argue over the week's soccer scores, while you and Mrs. Thomas . . . try not to argue over anything at all," he said with a wink.

"Vince—"

"No, no, Michael. I insist. You've already assured me everything is in place, and set to go. There is nothing left to do now but wait, and I would truly have to wonder about your state of mind, my friend, if you say you prefer to spend the time with us instead of with a beautiful young woman."

If Michael was upset over the perfunctory dismissal, it did not show. "Are you sure you don't need me?"

Giancarlo dragged his eyes away from Megan and frowned. "Of course I need you. I need you to phone the kitchen and order me a four-inch steak. And pasta—lots of pasta, and calamari, and grouper . . . When I *need* you, I'll send Gino to find you. Until then, relax. Enjoy."

Michael looked anything but relaxed. He hesitated another few moments, but when the conversation drifted into more small talk, he turned away to use the phone on his desk.

When he did so, the light he had been shielding with his body frame spilled more brightly on Megan's features, defining her face more clearly, removing the muted shadows and making her coloring more pronounced. Giancarlo, in the middle of a sentence, fell abruptly silent and stared into the startling emerald green of her eyes.

"Forgive me, Mrs. Thomas, but ... have we met somewhere before?"

Megan did not flinch, but she could feel the distinct beating of her heart as it crawled halfway up her throat. On that one otherwise unnoteworthy day so many months ago she had slipped into court to observe the preliminary motions against Vincent Giancarlo; in less than twenty minutes, his lawyers had made mincemeat out of the prosecutor's flimsy evidence. Leaving the courtroom in a flush of smug triumph, Giancarlo had passed close to where Megan sat. Worse still, a crush of reporters had been waiting for him in the corridor, crowding him inside the doors for the time it had taken his bodyguards to clear a path through. A matter of seconds, no more. Long enough for a man who reputedly went through mistresses like other men went through newspapers, to catch her staring at him and acknowledge her interest with a nod.

But there was no earthly way he could recall so trivial an encounter almost two years ago.

"I ... don't believe so, Mr...?"

He snapped out of his stance and took her hand in his again.

"How unforgivably rude! Michael is like a son to me, but sometimes his manners—" He shook his head in mock despair.

Michael overheard the exchange and tucked the phone under his chin, covering the mouthpiece with his hand. He looked intently at Megan for a moment before murmuring an apology and correcting the oversight.

"Mrs. Megan Thomas . . . Vincent Giancarlo."

Giancarlo beamed. "The pleasure is all mine, I assure you. And I must warn you, I rarely forget a face. If we have met somewhere before, I'll remember it eventually."

"All set," Michael said, hanging up the phone. He came around in front of the desk again and this time Megan did not miss the terse glance he gave Gino. "René has promised to outdo himself, and the private dining room is being prepared. Gino will take you down, Vince, and see that you have everything you need."

"Excellent. Excellent. Come along then, Eduardo, my stomach is rumbling like a volcano."

The Colombian did not have to be called twice. He stood and walked to the door without sparing more than a cursory nod in Megan's direction. Gino and the two bodyguards followed, the latter lingering by the door until Giancarlo joined them.

"I trust we will see more of each other, Mrs. Thomas."

She offered a lame smile and murmured something hopelessly inadequate; it was Michael who walked with them as far as the door to the lobby and stood watching until he was satisfied they had indeed gone in the direction of the restaurant. When he returned, Megan had moved over to stand by the window and was looking out over the busy street. She heard Michael close the door behind him, and she heard the subsequent soft click as the lock was eased into place.

His reflection was cast on the windowpane. He looked angry—furious, in fact, and she tensed herself for the confrontation she knew was inevitable. She let the curtain drop back over the window, but she could not turn to face him. Not just yet.

"I'm sorry. I didn't know you were busy."

"It was my own fault. I should have read the messages that were waiting for me at reception. Excuse me a minute, will you—I have to make a quick phone call."

His voice was cold and formal; a disturbing contrast to the warm and earnest warning he had given her earlier not to be late for their rendezvous.

He stabbed a few buttons on his telephone console and spoke quietly into the receiver, too quietly for Megan to have followed what he was saying, if she had wanted to listen. Something about guests and reservations...

When he finished, he hung up the phone, but did not move from the far side of the desk. Megan had stolen no more than a few quick glances, and even they came to an abrupt halt when she felt his eyes concentrate all their considerable power on her slender shoulders.

Megan closed her eyes. "Michael...the justice department knows all about Vincent Giancarlo's business dealings. They know he owns the casino and they know you work for him." Her voice faltered and she fell silent.

"Was that the something important you came to tell me?"

"Not entirely."

He was watching her, waiting, and she wished she had never laid eyes on Abner Hornsby, never opened herself to so much pain.

"The other morning on the beach...when we argued...you asked me if I was here strictly on vacation. I didn't answer you. I couldn't answer you because...because the truth of the matter is...I'm not just here for a holiday. I also didn't tell you the whole truth about my being a lawyer. I *am* a lawyer, but I work for the district attorney's office, and I'm here because they sent me. Well...*they* didn't actually send me—it was more of a request from a treasury department official—an anal-retentive agent by the name of Hornsby. He showed me a picture of you taken a few months ago with Giancarlo. It was badly blurred and I didn't recognize you, but apparently *he* thought I did the first time I saw it, and...and he thought it would expedite matters to simply send me down here so I could look at you in person."

A single, fat tear slid from the corner of her eye, wetting a shiny path all the way down to her chin.

"They only knew your name as Vallaincourt, you see, and it put them all in a frenzy when they discovered the name had no past history."

He drew a deep breath and expelled it slowly. "I gather that small oversight has now been rectified?"

Megan turned and met his eyes for the first time. "I didn't have much choice. I couldn't change my mind once I was here or refuse to cooperate. And I couldn't lie. As much as I wanted to, as much as I was tempted to, and as much as you have come to mean to me, I couldn't lie! They would have known something was wrong and then both of us would have been compromised. But this way... this way, at least it's out in the open and I can help you. Whatever it is, Michael, whatever you're involved in, I can help you. You're not like them, you never were. I'll do anything you want me to do, anything I *can* do to help you find a way out if you want it, as . . . as long as you don't ask me to lie for you."

Michael stared at her in silence, seeming to need an inordinate amount of time to digest her impassioned confession. He looked down at his hands and flexed them, then sent his eyes on a protracted glide along the length of her body.

"So," he murmured. "You want to help me."

Megan held her breath until she thought she would suffocate from the pressure.

"You come here on a...diverting little mission for the treasury department, at the behest of—what was your boss's name? Hornsby?"

"He isn't my boss. I was just doing him a favor. I didn't even want to come here in the first place! I had a quiet vacation planned in Cape Cod until . . . until . . ."

"Until you were persuaded to do this *favor* for Hornsby?" He pursed his lips consideringly. "And then, for whatever the reason, when you finished doing him your little favor, you felt compelled to come here and offer to do another one for me?"

"I want to help you, Michael," she said, her voice barely a whisper. "If you'll let me. But I can't unless you tell me what it is you're involved in, and I . . . I won't if it has anything to do with drugs."

"Such noble discrimination," he chided. "I thought a crime was a crime was a crime."

He took two measured steps toward her, his eyes commanding all her attention. "But you don't really believe it's drugs, do you?"

"I don't know what to believe. Drugs are the absolute worst thing I could think of off the top of my head, and . . . and there is Samosa. He's Colombian, isn't he? A natural association with drugs. And you can't tell me Giancarlo has any noble discriminations about *anything*."

Michael smiled crookedly. "No, I suppose he doesn't."

He was moving inexorably closer while Megan backed up, stumbling against the corner of a bookshelf as she sought to keep a safe distance between herself and Michael's anger.

"You could have asked, you know. You could have told me who you were and why you were here, and you could have just come right out and asked me what you wanted to know."

"W-would you have told me?"

Michael's eyes flickered down to the enticingly low vee of her neckline. "If you had chosen your moment right, it's possible I would have told you anything you wanted to know."

Megan fought an unexpected rush of tears. He was being deliberately cruel, taunting her with insinuations. "It wouldn't have made any difference. You are who you are and I am who I am. It never would have worked out, regardless of whether or not one of us could have been honest with the other."

"I thought it had been working rather well these past few days," he said with a frown, narrowing the gap between them with menacing ease. "But I guess that was all part of the game, too, wasn't it?"

"Game?"

"Come on, Megan, we're both adults. We enjoyed each other's company, each other's bodies. I must admit you played the part of the ingenue very well. The shy act was genuinely convincing. You almost had me making a damned fool of myself all over again."

Megan stopped and stared. "It wasn't an act! *I* meant everything I said, everything I did while we were together. The only thing I didn't mean to do was fall in love with you, but it happened and I'm not sorry. If *you* were the one who was just playing games, or if you still think this is some kind of a *ploy* to win your sympathy, well then . . . then you truly are a damned fool, because I could have loved you forever, and now you've just . . . just thrown it all away!"

Despite her efforts to block them, Megan's tears began to flow. Hot and fast, they splashed over her lashes and spilled down her cheeks. And she hated them. She hated them, and she hated him for seeing them. She hadn't cried like this since she was a little girl, but that was exactly how she was feeling now, how Michael was making her feel—helpless and vulnerable and hopelessly inadequate . . .

Michael's face had drained of some of the ruddy color. His hands reached haltingly out to her, and although she batted them away once, they returned with a perseverance she could feel as he cradled her face between them and forced her to look up into his eyes—eyes that were so blue they were painful to behold.

"Let me go!" she cried.

His eyes searched her face with a relentless hunger and his grip tightened. "Did you just say . . . you loved me?"

"I . . . don't love you," she insisted, although by now, neither of them believed it.

"And I don't love you, either," he said matter-of-factly. "And if I don't love you now, I guess I didn't really love you fifteen years ago."

Megan stopped struggling and stood perfectly still. What was he saying? What on earth was he saying? That he had felt the same way she had all those years ago?

"Funny thing, though," he mused. "It took me a long time to get over you. I had to leave, and I knew I had to forget you, but . . . I never really did. I tried, by God. I went through women like there was no tomorrow, but there was always something wrong with them. I didn't even know what that something was until the other day when I saw you in the casino."

"Michael, please don't—"

"I was flabbergasted. Just thinking you *looked* like you made me search through the registration slips. And when I found out it *was* you—"

Megan looked up. She had to know the truth.

He was waiting, and he gave her no reason to doubt him.

"When I kissed you in the parking lot, I was shaking like a schoolboy—I'm surprised you couldn't feel it. And on the dance floor? I don't know what I would have done if you hadn't gone with me . . . but you did, and I fell in love with you all over again . . . like a fool," he added softly.

Megan blinked. She raised a hand and dashed away the residue of her tears in a gesture so innocent and so stubbornly determined, that Michael almost smiled.

"But how can you still say you love me?" she challenged. "I betrayed you."

"You didn't betray me. I betrayed myself."

"*I* was the one who told them about you."

He sighed and brushed his thumbs across the fullness of her lower lip.

"I'm sure Hornsby and the others could have found out on their own. They just used you, and it wasn't very fair. I might just have to do something nice to them in return."

Megan's eyes widened. "Oh . . . no . . . Michael, you mustn't—"

He laughed suddenly and held her out to arm's length. "Mustn't what? Send someone to break their kneecaps? I think you've been watching too many gangster movies. We're a little more discreet these days."

Megan flushed. "That wasn't what I meant at all."

"Good, because we only break fingers, and the odd toe now and then."

"You're making fun of me," she said softly. "And this isn't a laughing matter."

"No, it isn't," he agreed, drawing her back into his arms. "But if I don't make fun of you, I might get angry all over again, and then neither one of us would be very amused."

She sighed miserably and buried her face in the crook of his neck. "You *are* angry. I can tell."

"You do seem to have put me somewhere between a rock and a hard place, if you'll pardon the cliché."

"Michael—" her voice was muffled, but the words were carefully articulated "—I *can* help you. I can place a call to New York tonight. Right now. I'll speak to the district attorney, Phil Levy—he's a good and fair man. He'll know what to do. There are witness protection programs—"

Michael tilted his head back, forcing her to come out of hiding. "Witness protection? Witness . . . as in grand jury testimony?"

"As in immunity from prosecution. It's the only way to be truly free from the Abner Hornsbys of the world . . . and the Vincent Giancarlos."

Michael, in the face of her heartrending sincerity, looked infuriatingly amused.

"Do you know how many witnesses have lived to testify against Vincent?"

"You would be protected—"

"I would be dead," he stated flatly. "And you've taken a big leap in logic by deducing I would even entertain the idea of appearing before a grand jury."

"Are you saying you definitely wouldn't testify?"

"Not on a dime, Megan. Sorry if it shatters any illusions you have about my being a noble and honorable fellow, but the harsh reality of it is that I like living, I like breathing, and I like being able to walk down a street without having to look over my shoulder every time someone sneezes. You can't do any of those things from the bottom of the Hudson River."

"Then we have a problem, don't we," she said quietly.

"I suppose we do."

While Michael considered the provocative flush in her cheeks and the spark of defiance darkening the green of her eyes, the silence stretched and grew until it throbbed between them like a third heartbeat.

"Don't discount your importance to me so quickly, Megan. I meant it when I said I loved you, and I mean it when I say I will probably love you until the day I die. If that doesn't make you damned important to me—"

Megan rose swiftly onto her tiptoes, startling him by pressing a fierce kiss over his mouth. "You are every bit as important to me, Michael, and I have no intention of giving up on you so easily."

She kissed him again, winning no response for a long, torturous moment, but then she felt the gust of an oath break hotly between her lips and his arms circled her waist, as he pulled her into the heat of his body.

"I knew you were trouble," he muttered huskily. "I knew it at the diner, and I knew it on the dance floor...! I should never have touched you. I shouldn't touch you now."

But instead of pushing her away, his hands brought her even closer, crushing her to him so that she could not help but be aware of the passions raging within him. The breathless moan, deep in her throat, made her conscious of her own soaring, primitive emotions, and of the shameless desire that flared hotter with each thrust of his tongue, each tremor that caused his hunger to grow bolder.

Their mouths parted for as long as it took them to look deeply into each other's eyes, then they were together again, their breaths and pulse beats quickening with a blind recklessness.

His hands slid up beneath the sleek fabric of her dress and she heard his soft moan as he encountered the warm scrap of silk she wore underneath. A dizzying rush of exquisite pleasure assailed her as his fingers stole beneath the border of delicate lace. He knew exactly where to touch her to elicit the first shivered gasp, and he knew exactly how to tease her flesh into further eroding her most basic senses of right and wrong.

"Michael . . . we can't. We mustn't."

"I don't know about you, but I'm getting tired of hearing what I can't, what I mustn't do. If there is one thing I absolutely should do, and want to do, it's this."

His fingers pressed deeper and the sweet, hot spiral of surrender sent her melting against him. His mouth was there to stifle her cries, caressing her into throaty moans of capitulation even as her resistance crumbled before a sinfully resolute pair of hands.

Megan's knees buckled and she did not even try to deter him as he swept her into his arms and carried her to the couch. Together they sank onto the thick, plush cushions, where he swiftly raised the hem of her skirt and pushed it into a crush of silk beneath her arms.

Seeing the all but transparent camisole she had so carefully chosen to wear for an evening of seduction, the blue of his eyes gleamed with appreciation, and his smile was rakishly approving.

"This *was* for me, I hope," he murmured, his fingertips tracing lightly over and around the tautening peaks of her breasts. The satin sheath was almost as erotic a stimulant as his feather-light strokes, and Megan strained upward, her eyes fixed imploringly on the blatant sensuality of his mouth.

Reading a desire that mirrored his own, Michael bent his dark head and took the puckered nipple into his mouth, satin and all. Megan arched against him, her fingers clawing into the lush black waves of his hair. His mouth lavished rivers of flaming sensation on her flesh, dampening the satin, cooling it where it clung to her fevered skin, adding the further torment of ice to the growing fire within her.

The suckling intimacy paused long enough for his hand to chase a skittering ripple of anticipation lower, pursuing it to the filmy triangle of satin and lace that barely covered the downy vee between her thighs.

"As for this," he said, his composure slipping noticeably as he bared the porcelain smoothness of her hip. "This—" his fingers brushed reverently over the golden tangle of curls "—just isn't fair, Counselor."

"If there is a choice between playing fair and winning," she whispered, quoting his own philosophy, "I prefer to win every time."

He glanced up, momentarily humbled by the pride and love shining in her eyes. He drank in the soft pink flush that stained her cheeks, and the moist, slightly parted lips that brought all manner of heady fantasies to mind. He seared the sight of them on his memory, knowing he would want to recall them until the instant he drew his last breath.

His hand curled around the cool heat of the satin and he tore it in his impatience to be rid of it. Megan gasped at the sudden freedom and brazenly wrapped her long, slender limbs around him, half laughing, half sobbing as her flesh met the impediment of his own clothing.

Jacket and shirt were summarily pushed off his shoulders, stripped from the muscular expanse of his chest and arms. Cursing because he had to abandon her to shrug both garments to the floor, Michael's hands clashed momentarily with Megan's over his belt and zipper, but he obligingly retreated when it became quite clear she could manage on her own.

The air hissed softly from between his teeth as her cool fingers closed around him. His head bowed to her breast again, but this time, he was barely able to taste the warmth of her flesh before a muffled groan sent his lips upward, seeking out the tender curve of her shoulder. Drunk on the fragrance of her skin and hair, he slid his hands beneath her hips and pressed himself urgently into the moist, undulant haven.

Eagerly, Megan strained to meet him, but even as he began to sink into her, the cushions beneath them crushed downward, their plushness absorbing most of the impact of his thrust.

Michael shifted his weight, groaning as he tried again with little more success.

He lifted her against him, holding her secure as he reversed their positions on the couch. Seated now, he lowered her slowly over him, her knees straddling his hips, quivering with uncertainty.

Megan instinctively held herself back as she felt the enormity of his need, but as he slid deeper and deeper within her, she let herself go limp, let herself trust the skill and guidance of his hands. Inch by inch, he filled her, swelling and stretching within her until their bodies became as closely bound as they had ever imagined being. Closer still, and they groaned in breathless unison, their mouths joining, sharing the pleasure.

Megan's hands clutched at his shoulders and she had to draw upon every ounce of willpower she possessed not to thrust and thrust and thrust herself against him. She could feel the encroaching shivers of ecstasy beginning to undermine her composure and she fought them as best she could. She tried to focus on the lean lines of his face, but that made it worse, not better, for she could see the effect her paralyzing arousal was having on him.

Megan arched her back slowly, urging a subtle pressure where it was wanted most. She said his name on a gasp as she felt his lips pressed into the hollow of her throat; she heard the gasp turn into a raw, ragged cry as his hands began to move her to the rhythm of their wildly beating hearts.

Michael felt her deep contractions grasping him, gripping him tighter. He weathered the initial waves of her orgasm with the aplomb of a statesman, but when the drenching surges of heat began to flood his senses and the sleek, slippery demands of her body began to scoff at the restraint of his hands, he threw all thoughts of temperance aside and drove into her with all of the power and passion at his command.

It wasn't enough. It would never be enough and Michael realized this even as the pleasure exploded within him. Greedily, hungrily he thrust into her, knowing these few moments of unutterable bliss would have to last him a lifetime. He had lost her once and that loss had been like an emptiness inside him for fifteen years. He would, in all probability, lose her again in a matter of a few hours, a result of his own stupidity.

But here and now, she belonged to him, and desperately, almost angrily, he prolonged her shuddering pleasure as long as humanly possible, wanting his memories all to be of Megan—of her stunning beauty, her fiery passion, her broken cries of disbelieving joy. Here and now, he loved her as much as a man could possibly love a woman, and the temptation was very real, very palpable to simply run with her, as fast and far away as they could go. But he knew it wasn't possible. Just as he knew it wasn't possible to think of any kind of a future with Megan Worth after tonight.

After tonight, she would undoubtedly hate him as much as a woman could possibly hate a man.

· 12

THE COLOR REMAINED HIGH in Megan's cheeks as she strove in vain to repair the damage to her hair and clothes. Without a comb or brush, the blond mass tumbled around her shoulders as if it had been caught in a windstorm. And her dress—the material was puckered and wrinkled beyond any modest hope of escaping notice.

Michael's hands paused in their own clumsy reparations as he glanced over and saw her frowning at the torn scrap of her panties.

"You'll be all right as long as you don't bend over to pick up any shiny new pennies," he advised, his attempt at humor only causing the blush to ebb and flow in her complexion.

"I feel naked," she said uncomfortably.

"You look beautiful."

Megan averted her eyes and pulled at the hem of her skirt, trying in vain to win extra inches that simply were not there.

Michael shrugged into his jacket and came up behind her. As much as he tried, he could not resist the temptation to touch her, to bring her warmth into his arms again. Gently he swept aside the heavy silken mass of her hair and placed a kiss on the smooth nape of her neck.

"I'm sorry if you feel uncomfortable. The blame is all mine, and I accept it fully."

"It isn't all yours," she amended with a sigh. "I suppose I could have stopped you if I'd wanted to."

"Really? At what point, precisely?"

She sighed again as his lips continued to nuzzle her neck. Since it shouldn't have surprised her that he knew how helpless she was in his arms, why did it still have the capacity to surprise her? Then again, how often in her life had she been in love to know exactly how she was supposed to feel or react?

"Michael . . . what are we going to do?"

His lips stopped teasing the fine hairs at her nape and pressed a kiss into the golden mass at her crown. "That depends. Did you mean what you said when you told me you would do anything I asked?"

"Of course I meant it," she said, but when she would have turned around to face him, he planted his hands firmly on her shoulders, preventing it.

"And if I wanted you to do something for me, would you do it without asking me a lot of questions?"

She felt her initial flush of warmth desert her. "That depends . . . on what you want me to do."

"Nothing illegal," he assured her wryly. "Nothing remotely compromising."

Megan's heartbeat quickened. "What do you want me to do?"

"First, I want you to tell me who your contact is here at the hotel."

"My contact?"

He felt her shoulders stiffen and he smiled. "I'm sure the treasury department didn't send you down here on your own. And I'm only asking because I want to know if he can get you and your cousin off the island tonight."

"Off the—!" She turned despite the efforts of his hands and body to block her. "Why would we want to get off the island?"

"Megan—you said you wouldn't ask any questions," he reminded her sternly. "If I gave you too many answers, you'd find yourself right alongside me between that rock and hard place."

Megan studied his face intently. He was protecting her from something...becoming an accessory after the fact, perhaps...something. And because he wanted her off the island tonight, it must have something to do with Giancarlo's sudden appearance.

"I'm not leaving."

"Yes you are."

"No," she shook her head. "I'm not."

Michael squared his jaw and scowled, but far from having the desired effect, it only made Megan's temper bristle to the surface.

"Furthermore, I don't much like the way you're dismissing me, as if I'm incompetent, utterly useless, and incapable of dealing with the harsh realities of the situation—*whatever they might be*."

"Megan...I asked you to trust me, and you said you would."

"I do trust you. But I also love you and I'm hoping the two things combined haven't clouded my judgment entirely."

He drew a deep breath and released it slowly. "They haven't. My word on it, Megan, it will all be explained and straightened out for you in the morning. No more secrets, no more mysteries."

Megan's frown deepened, but she suspected she would not be able to push him much further. He was promising explanations in the morning and she had to believe him. This time she *had* to believe him and she would see that he kept his word.

"I'm still not leaving the island."

Michael groaned and closed his eyes briefly. "Then you'll at least get the hell out of this hotel and check yourself and your cousin into another one, preferably on the other side of town."

"Why?"

"Because I'm asking you to, dammit. I'm also asking you again—who is your contact here?"

Megan capitulated, but grudgingly. "His name is Dallas. That's what he calls himself, anyway. I don't know if it's his first name, his last name, or his nickname. I just know him as Dallas."

"Fair enough. How do you get in touch with him if you need him?"

Megan hesitated again, not quite able to bring herself to tell him about the bracelet. She had felt foolish putting it on at the time, and to Michael it would seem abysmally James Bondish.

"I don't. I mean, I didn't. He got in touch with me."

Michael's eyes narrowed. "What does he look like? Describe him to me."

"Tall, heavyset. White hair. He has a thick Texan accent and wears a jewelry store on his fingers and around his neck."

He nodded. "I know the one you mean. And he's it, as far as you know?"

"Yes. But why are you so worried about my safety? I'm not in any danger."

"Not directly, anyway. But I am. Your presence here poses a distinct risk to me."

"You!"

"The first thing you learn in this business is never to let anyone see you have a weakness. Giancarlo saw you in here tonight, and knows you're my weakness. The second, equally important rule has to do with never taking anything for granted. Just the fact that you knew who Giancarlo was the moment you walked into this office poses a double risk—to you for being able to identify him, to me for keeping company with an assistant district attorney."

"But he doesn't know—"

"Don't kid yourself—he'll know by morning. I saw the way he was looking at you, and he isn't the type to let a beautiful woman slip through his fingers."

Megan's stubbornness drained away in a rush as the echo of Giancarlo's words collided with Michael's.

"I rarely forget a face. If we have met, I'll remember it eventually."

"Will you, for heaven's sake, give me a little latitude on this?"

"What?"

"I'm not accustomed to these feelings of responsibility you seem to be rousing in me. I'm not used to having to worry about anyone's neck but my own."

"*Are* you worried?" she asked solemnly. "And I don't just mean about me."

"I'm plenty worried," he murmured, taking her face in his hands. "I'm worried what might happen in the next minute or two if you don't stop looking at me like that—or have you forgotten you *are* half-naked beneath this flimsy bit of nothing?"

Megan melted into his kiss, uncertain of whether she was left feeling better or worse from its effects.

"I won't be put off so easily by your feeble attempts to distract me," she warned softly. "I'll change hotels, if that's what you want me to do, but you won't be able to keep me away forever, Michael. I'll be back. One way or another, I *will* be back, and between us, we will find a way to work this out."

Without waiting for his response, she turned and walked back to the desk, rather proud of herself for doing so without her knees collapsing beneath her. She could feel the heat of his eyes on her and she knew it would never be as easy as she had made it sound. There was a wall between them—a wall labeled *justice*, with a right side and a wrong side to it and it still separated them.

She retrieved her shoes from where they had been abandoned beside the desk. A stolen glance showed her that Michael was off guard and uncertain what to say to do next, and it looked good on him for a change.

In the morning, when he explained what had to be explained, it would be *his* turn to trust *her*. She was a damned good lawyer and she would find a breach in that wall somehow. If Phil or anyone else in the department had any qualms about the ethics of her helping Michael Vallaincourt, well, they could just take their precious job and their ethics and—

Michael's head turned sharply toward the door, his hand lifting in a sign for caution the same instant Megan heard a noise in the outer office. Someone was outside the door. A shadow had sliced across the narrow strip of light running along the threshold.

The brass knob began to turn, very slowly, as if it was being tested to see if it was locked.

Michael moved swiftly to the desk and slid the top drawer open. He was reaching for the gleaming black grip of a 9 mm Beretta when a hand knocked softly on the door.

"Mikey—you in there?"

It was Gino.

Michael's hand relaxed and he slid the drawer closed again.

"Just a minute." He met Megan's startled gaze—she had seen the gun and the change that had come over his features. It was the same change she had seen that first morning on the beach, all roguish charm and good humor one moment, cool and deadly intent the next.

Michael walked to the door and unlocked it.

"What is it?"

Gino tilted his head slightly to see past Michael's shoulder. "Dinner meeting is over. Vince wants to see you."

Michael swore under his breath. He glanced at his wristwatch and swore again. "All right. I'll have to take Megan back to her room first, and then—"

"Ah...I don't think that's such a good idea. He wants to see you right away. He's not too happy about a couple of things he found out over dinner, and if you're smart, you'd use the little bit of time you have to do some quick thinking."

"What things? What's wrong?" Megan blurted and displeasure flashed in Michael's eyes. She had supposed Gino to be Michael's friend, but Gino was also employed by Vincent Giancarlo. His loyalties and obligations would be to Giancarlo first, superseding any feelings of friendship he might have toward Michael.

Dear God, it was getting more and more complicated by the minute. She needed time to think. Time *alone* to think everything through.

She reached for her purse and cast one last glance around the room to see if anything had been left behind. At the last moment, she became aware she was still clutching the fistful of torn silk, and, flushing self-consciously, she stuffed it into her small leather bag.

"You don't have to worry about me, Michael, I can take myself back to my room."

"I'm . . . sorry, Megan. I'll get away as soon as I can."

"Business before pleasure," she said brightly, smiling for Gino's benefit as she walked to the door. She was almost past the two men when she felt Michael's hand on her arm and heard him fall into step beside her. He did not look back, but Megan knew he was alert to Gino's eyes and ears following them.

"Don't do anything hasty until you hear from me," he murmured.

Megan stopped at the outer door. She looked up into his lean, handsome face, and her smile was only slightly forced.

"You know I'll wait was long as it takes."

She kissed him in spite of Gino's watchfulness, then left before her bravado deserted her completely. For once she was thankful for the ever-present crowds in the lobby, hurrying into their midst without a care for the curious looks her appearance earned. She knew Michael stood at the door watching her, as she crossed the marbled foyer and left the main building, wanting only to feel the cool night air on her burned skin.

The bungalows on either side of hers were rocking with music and laughter. Judging by the sound, the party on the beach was still in full swing, as well.

She fumbled blindly for her key, noting irritably that the bulb outside their door must have burned out, for the little vined enclave was nearly pitch-black. It took two fruitless stabs in the darkness before her efforts were rewarded by the sound of the key releasing the lock.

She heard a faint scuffling sound from inside, followed by what could have been a choked-off scream. But before she could react, the door was yanked open and she found herself staring at the barrel of a snub-nosed automatic.

"COME IN. Come in, Mrs. Thomas . . . or should I say, Miss Worth. Come in and join us," Vincent Giancarlo said, at ease in the flowered divan. The bodyguard Megan had seen earlier in Michael's office was by the door, holding the gun. A second, brutish-looking thug was struggling to recapture the writhing, kicking form of her cousin, while cursing viciously over a bitten, bleeding finger.

"Do come and join us, Miss Megan Worth, assistant district attorney for the borough of Manhattan. My, my, my, I see you must have been enjoying your dinner very much. A pity the evening had to end so abruptly."

Megan ignored the leering inspection he gave her wrinkled clothes and tousled hair. She concentrated very hard on curbing the impulse to scream, but the effort took every last scrap of energy she had. There was none to spare on thinking about Michael; barely enough in reserve to force a dry rasp out of her throat.

"What are you doing here?" she asked. "What do you want?"

"I think . . . I should be the one asking you that question, should I not?"

"I don't know what you mean."

"Oh, come now, Miss Worth. You may have been able to dupe Michael with those big green eyes of yours, but me? I don't like coincidences in any way, shape, or form."

"And I don't like your presence here in any way, shape, or form. Now will you kindly tell that animal to get his hands off my cousin!"

Giancarlo smiled blithely. "His hands will stay exactly where they are until I get the answers to a few questions. And if I don't like those answers, well—" He lifted a hand and Shari gasped, her struggles stopping at once. The thug had wrapped his arm around her waist and was holding her pinned at an awkward angle over his other arm—an arm that was thick enough to snap her spine with little or no effort.

"Let her go," Megan cried aghast. "She isn't involved in any of this."

"Implying that you are...involved in something, that is?"

"I'm implying nothing," she countered hotly. "And I resent your intrusion. Forcible entry and confinement is a criminal offence."

He threw back his handsome head and laughed. "I can see why Michael was attracted to you. You have a fine sense of humor, Miss Worth, and you remain calm under pressure. So very important these days. Me? I like a calm woman. She can usually size up a situation right away and know what is the best recourse for her. Do you know what the best recourse is for you, Miss Worth?"

"Why don't you tell me," she spat.

"The truth, Miss Worth. The whole truth and nothing but the truth—isn't that how it goes?" His grin broadened and he rubbed a tanned forefinger along the side of his nose. "I told you, I never forget a face. Most especially not a beautiful one. And definitely not one with eyes the color of fine emeralds. That was what caught my attention in the courthouse, Miss Assistant District Attorney. Eyes like those, and a body made for pleasure...imagine my disappointment when I learned you were with the prosecutor's office. I was hoping perhaps you were a reporter, one who might have wanted an exclusive interview."

"Am I supposed to be flattered?" she asked coldly.

"Would it hurt to smooth a little oil on an old man's ruffled feathers?" he countered affably.

"What is it you want, Mr. Giancarlo?"

"I already told you—the truth. Why did you come to the islands?"

Megan debated her answer for a moment, but a quick look at the wide-eyed fear on Shari's face convinced her that the truth was indeed the only way out.

"I came here to identify Michael."

"Identify Michael? What do you mean, identify Michael?"

It wasn't what Giancarlo had been expecting to hear and she took some satisfaction in seeing his temporary confusion.

"No one in the justice department seemed to know who Michael Vallaincourt was. For some reason, they thought I recognized him from a blurred picture, and for the sake of expediency, sent me down here to attempt a positive identification." Slowly, Megan felt a measure of control returning, and allowing her to detach herself from her emotions, just as she was able to do it in a courtroom. "The name Vallaincourt," she added, her voice tainting the explanation with sarcasm, "has no history. You also should have known a face without a name would have drawn someone's attention, sooner or later."

The explanation was so simple and so basic, she could see it would be harder to sell as the truth.

Giancarlo steepled his long fingers together and propped them under his chin. "I see. And because you were old school chums—I presume that much of your story is still true—you would have known Michael by his real name—Antonacci. So. You came, you saw, you were able to give the picture-takers a name for their files. What else were you supposed to find out for them?"

"There was nothing else. That was it."

"Nothing else? No other reason why they wanted to put you into his bed?"

Megan flushed red with anger. "No one ordered me into his bed."

"It wasn't part of your *assignment*? You weren't supposed to get close to him, to find out about the plates?"

"Plates? What plates?"

Giancarlo laughed. "You're not very convincing, and you're not being very cooperative."

He lifted his hand in the direction of the man holding Shari, but a voice from behind Megan's shoulder stopped him.

"She's telling the truth. She doesn't know anything about the plates."

The sound of Michael's quiet baritone caused Megan to jump and whirl around in surprise. He was standing just inside the door, his hands in his pockets, his shoulders propped nonchalantly against the wall. It was not possible for Giancarlo to have missed seeing him there, the two men were in direct sight of each other.

"You say she knows nothing," Giancarlo said. "But I suggest your judgment might be somewhat clouded at the moment."

"There is nothing wrong with my judgment," Michael said. "Yours, perhaps, for jumping to conclusions."

Giancarlo's eyes glittered ominously. "You know I don't like surprises, Michael. Why didn't you tell me who she was and why she was here?"

"Because I wasn't sure myself until an hour ago. All I knew up to then was that she was a lawyer here on vacation."

"And now? What do you know now?"

"I know that if you had skipped the strong-arm routine and talked to me first, I could have told you she knew nothing and that we had nothing to worry about."

Giancarlo rose to his feet. He clasped his hands behind his back and paced the length of the couch before turning and glaring first at Michael, then at Megan.

"Who sent you here? Who was so curious to know Michael's identity?"

Megan was still reeling from Michael's sudden appearance, and bewildered by his behavior. He was giving a very good impression of a man who had just returned from completing a distasteful but necessary chore, and she was not sure what she should say or if he would want her to say anything at all.

"She told me it was your old friend from the treasury department," Michael supplied dryly, startling Megan into staring at him again. "Abner Hornsby."

"Hornsby! That little boll weevil?"

"A weevil, but one with an uncanny sense of timing, wouldn't you say?"

Giancarlo slammed his fist into his cupped hand. "Damn! He must have caught wind, somehow, that we were taking delivery of the merchandise tonight."

Michael shook his head. "I don't think so. I think he's just poking around in the dark."

Giancarlo's dark eyes went from Michael to Megan, then back to Michael. "Is this another hunch, or do you know this for sure?"

"Let's just say, after this last hour together, I don't think the counselor would have held out on me, or kept any secrets from me . . . would you, sweetheart?"

Megan recoiled from the hand Michael held out to pat her cheek. She was staring at him in shock, cringing from more than just his touch. He seemed amused by her response. He was smiling—actually *smiling* as he strolled past her into the sitting room.

Giancarlo shook his head and grinned. "Ah, Michael, Michael. To be twenty years younger and so sure of myself, not to mention having the same inexhaustible powers of persuasion. You must have been exceptionally convincing in your role this time. Look at the poor girl—you had her believing you were almost human."

Michael shrugged. "She had her eyes open all the time. Well, most of the time, anyway."

Giancarlo's grin broadened into a leer. "Maybe I should have left the two of you alone a while longer?"

"God, no. As it is, it'll take a month to get the taste of all that patience and sweetness out of my mouth."

Megan felt a wave of faintness sweep through her and she was grateful for the support of the wall. Was it possible it had all been an act? The vows of love, the tender endearments, the promises... Had Michael simply been using his charm, using *her* to find out what the justice department knew?

"Do you feel any better?" he was asking Giancarlo. "Can you relax now?"

"I never relax. That's why I'm still here today while others are either behind bars or six feet under. But if you say I have nothing to worry about, then I'll take your word for it. Tell me though, did she happen to mention if she was alone in this venture, or if there were any other ferrets sniffing around?"

Megan glanced sidelong at Michael, her last flicker of hope crushed brutally under his callous smile.

"Only one other that she knows about. A ferret by the name of Dallas. I've noticed him around—nothing to worry about."

"You keep saying that, but I do worry, Michael," said Giancarlo, his grin hardening as the muscles stretched taut in his jaw. "I have waited a very long time to get my hands on this merchandise. Too long to discount even a buffoon like Abner Hornsby."

Michael shrugged. "If it bothers you, I'll have Gino take care of it."

"No. Not Gino. You take care of it yourself, Michael. I don't want anymore unpleasant surprises."

"Gino is a good man. You've never questioned his ability before."

"I've never carried ten million dollars around with me, either. Maybe it's making me a little prickly. Maybe it's making us all a little prickly."

Megan thought furiously. Ten million dollars! What could possibly be worth so much money? She tried to think back over everything Hornsby had told her, but all she could hear was the echo of Giancarlo's voice telling Michael to "take care of Dallas."

It sickened her to look at Michael and realize that all the time he had been making love to her, he had felt nothing. Nothing then, nothing now. She was standing here in her torn and wrinkled clothing, a source of rich amusement for his cold, indifferent blue eyes.

Giancarlo finally broke the tension-filled silence with an impatient sigh. "We have to be at the airfield by three a.m. We now have two more small worries to deal with before we can leave."

"Neither one of them knows anything that can hurt us," Michael said matter-of-factly. "We can keep them here, under guard, for a few hours, then put them on the first plane out in the morning."

"A viable option," Giancarlo agreed. "We will all be gone by then anyway, so it makes no difference who they choose to run crying to. Still—" he crooked a finger at Megan and his eyes glittered shrewdly "—I think I prefer to keep this one with us. If everything goes as planned, the worst she will have to endure is a long walk home. On the other hand, if something . . . unexpected . . . happens, we will all feel better with a little extra insurance."

"You don't trust my security arrangements?" Michael asked quietly.

"I trust you with my life," Giancarlo insisted. "What is even more important, *campadre*, is that I trust you with *your* life. But for the sake of everyone's pride, let's just say I would like the pleasure of Miss Worth's company a while longer."

Michael looked as if he could have argued the decision further—and for those few seconds, a flicker of hope sputtered to life in Megan's breast. It died when she saw him shrug again and reach into his pocket for one of his thin black cigars.

"It's your call," he said.

Shari, her mouth frozen shut with terror up until now, could hold herself back no longer. In a burst of energetic thrashing, she managed to wrench herself out of her captor's arms and launch herself halfway across the room.

"You bastard!" she shrieked. "You coldhearted, unfeeling, uncaring—"

The rest was lost to a garbled breath as her mouth was clamped shut again beneath a roughly callused hand. In response to an annoyed glance from Giancarlo, she was lifted bodily and carried squirming toward the bedroom.

"What are you going to do to her?" Megan cried, starting forward in a panic.

Another signal from Giancarlo caused the man with the gun to block Megan's path with the outthrust threat of a hard-muscled arm.

"Your friend will be subdued under a few pounds of heavy-duty twine," Giancarlo said dryly. "But otherwise left quite unharmed, I assure you. As for yourself, unless you relish the thought of walking twenty miles in stiletto heels, I suggest you take the opportunity to change into something more, ah, appropriate. My bodyguard Pauli will go with you to help you make your choice, if you like, or just to see that you don't try to do anything foolish."

A steely hand gripped her elbow and began steering her to her own room. Megan submitted to the brutish manhandling, but when she drew abreast of Michael, she could not stop herself from drawing back and searching his face for a hint of something . . . anything.

"Why?" she asked softly. "Just tell me why."

His eyes were like two flat chips of blue glass. "You had best dress warmly. It's going to be a long night."

Pauli tugged on her arm, snorting disdainfully as she stumbled against him. Righting herself, Megan jerked her arm out of his grasp and walked ahead of him into her bedroom.

For a moment, she stood in the gloom, too enraged, too numb, too confused to do more than fight back the rush of emotions that were squeezing her heart. She didn't understand what was happening. She didn't understand where it had all gone wrong, or why. She had been so sure he had loved her. She had seen it so clearly in his eyes . . .

"Come on," Pauli growled. "We ain't got all night."

Moving woodenly, Megan found a sweatshirt and track pants in a drawer, tennis socks and shoes in the closet. An attempt to close herself into the bathroom was prevented by a large booted foot.

Gritting her teeth through a renewed flush of resentment, Megan turned her back to the half-open door and quickly stripped off the wrinkled dress. She would have liked to take a hot shower and scour herself with a coarse bristle brush, but she doubted if even then she would feel clean. At least she was warmer in the tracksuit, and a few extra moments with a hairbrush made her feel less like a wild woman, less vulnerable to their sly stares.

It was when she gave herself a final passing glance in the mirror that she stopped and looked sharply at her own reflection. She was pale beneath her light tan; her eyes were red-rimmed, the green dark and brittle. Her lips were raw inside from her teeth savaging them, and her fingers trembled visibly as she raised them to her cheek. It was a far cry from the woman she had seen in the mirror a few brief days ago.

She was losing it. She was so busy feeling sorry for herself, she was forgetting who she was, who she should be. Okay, so something big was happening tonight; something bigger than even Hornsby had suspected. If Michael had lied about everything else, he might also have lied about the "merchandise" not being drugs. But Giancarlo had mentioned *plates*. What kind of plates were worth ten million dollars, and worth enough to bring Giancarlo to the island in person?

"Okay, Miss America—" Pauli leaned inside the door and scowled "—time's up."

Megan glared at him. Heavy-featured and obviously not familiar with the benefits of a strong deodorant, he would have been perfectly typecast for an old black-and-white Cagney film. Megan brushed past him and, with a new purposefulness in her stride, returned to the sitting room.

Giancarlo was standing by the patio doors; Michael had already gone, leaving in his wake the faintly aromatic scent of his cigar smoke.

"Very practical, Miss Worth," Giancarlo nodded. "And not one to senselessly waste time—another attribute to be admired in a woman. Shall we go?"

Megan folded her arms over her chest. "I have no intentions of going anywhere with you until I have had a chance to speak with my cousin and am assured she is unhurt."

Pauli grunted and reached out as if to grab her by the arm and drag her forcibly from the room. He was forestalled by a quick look from Giancarlo.

"No. It is a reasonable request. And if it saves us the necessity of carrying her everywhere we go, it is well worth a minute of extra time." Irritably, he peered at his watch. "One minute, Miss Worth. Exactly."

Megan wanted to run, but she forced herself to walk calmly across the sitting room and into the far bedroom.

Shari had been bound hand and foot and bundled onto the bed. her mouth was taped and her eyes were huge beneath the mop of tousled red curls. Megan was conscious of Pauli's strong odor in proximity to her, so there wasn't much she could say or do other than to try to relieve some of the fear in Shari's eyes.

"You'll be all right," Megan promised. "And so will I. They have nothing to gain by hurting either one of us."

Shari blinked—an attempt to hold back tears, Megan suspected, and she offered what she hoped would pass for a smile of encouragement.

"Just think what a story this will make for your next novel."

The hand was at her elbow again, pulling her away from the door. Despite her resolve to think and watch and listen with every one of the considerable skills she had honed over her years as a public defender and a prosecutor, Megan was shaking inside. Each step that carried her away from the relative safety of the bungalow echoed the leaden emptiness in her heart; each breath she drew for courage only filled her with an unshakable feeling that something was going to go terribly wrong.

14

AN HOUR LATER, three gleaming black cars left the parking lot of the Privateer and sped along the darkened highway to the tiny village of West End. On the outskirts of the village—if four stores and a row of tumbledown shacks qualified as such—was a private airfield that had been built on a wide, jutting finger of land. Constructed during World War II, it had been used mainly to ferry supplies from the mainland to the naval recreational base that had been built a mile away, on the north shore. The base had been closed down in the late fifties.

The adjacent airfield had been abandoned as well, left a victim of the wind-driven sand and salt spray. The runway was pitted and the shoulders had eroded with age and a vengeful Mother Nature. At one end, the ocean pounded relentlessly at the remnants of a stone retaining wall, the spray shooting across the tarmac to render it a slippery, shiny black. At the other end, perilously less than a mile away, the skeleton of a rotted control tower was all but swallowed behind a wall of encroaching trees.

A pilot had to be very good, or very motivated to land a plane there in full daylight. In the pitch darkness, with only a narrow thread of lights to guide his way, a man had to be mad.

The fact that there were lights, however, was the first clue that the airfield was not as deserted as it had first appeared. It was, in fact, one of the busiest places on the island at certain times—nights, mostly—and for the transportation of *certain* cargo. A smuggler's paradise, well maintained without seeming to be, efficiently ignored by the well-paid local police.

The three Mercedes prowled to a halt near the edge of the trees. Megan was riding in the rearmost car, forced to share Michael's taut silence as well as the oppressive company of three henchmen. Gino Romani rode with Giancarlo and his personal guard, while the stubby Colombian Eduardo Samosa, and his men occupied the third car.

With the exception of the one guard left to stand watch beside Megan's car, the others were dispatched along the tarmac, their silhouettes barely discernible in the utter darkness.

Megan was mildly surprised, but glad to be alone. Everything was happening too fast and she needed some time with the sound of her own heartbeat as her only distraction.

She had stopped trying to remember signs she should have seen in Michael's behavior, discrepancies in his moods and manners. There hadn't been any. She had fallen headlong in love with him, just as she had fifteen years ago, and had been given just as little warning before the bottom dropped out.

How could those hands, those lips have duped her so cunningly? How could his eyes have glowed with such honest emotion one moment and emptied of all humanity the next? How could he have loved her so unselfishly, so *passionately* and then dismissed her as if she were no more important than a dirty rag?

It wasn't possible.

Michael had lit another cigar and his outline was distinguishable from the others by the occasional glow of ash from the tip. Gino was nearby, lounging watchfully against the hood of the Mercedes. Samosa and Giancarlo stood to one side engrossed in conversation—mostly one-sided, to judge by the latter's generous hand gestures and frequent rumbles of laughter.

Megan leaned her forehead against the cool glass of the window, unable to keep her gaze from wandering back to Michael each time she forced it away.

She did not know the time, or exactly how long they had been waiting in the silence and darkness. She wished she could have lowered the windows, but the car had power controls and the rear doors and window had been closed and locked when the others had gotten out. The driver's window had been left open a crack, barely enough to rid the car of the stale odor of male bodies, and to afford her occasional snatches of overheard conversation.

As tense and frightening as her own predicament was, she could not help thinking of Shari, bound and gagged back in the bungalow. She hoped fervently that Giancarlo was a man of his word. Would her cousin ever forgive her for not telling the truth from the outset? Would she ever forgive herself for knowingly or unknowingly placing Shari in such danger?

And Dallas. What had her carelessness cost him?

After they had left the bungalow, she had been taken to Giancarlo's suite of rooms and put under close

guard. Neither Michael nor Gino had reappeared for
more than an hour—plenty of time, she supposed, to
have found Dallas and . . . and taken care of him. She
had not been able to meet Michael's eyes when he had
eventually joined them in the suite. She had kept her
gaze averted, all but defying him to glance in her direction. He hadn't.

Some slight, nervous change in the stance of the men
outside caused Megan to hold her breath and listen. A
faint, very faint droning overhead signaled the approach of the anxiously awaited aircraft. A switch was
thrown and parallel rows of evenly spaced lamps
blinked on, rippling down either side of the runway like
falling dominoes.

It was still a few minutes more before Megan could
hear the engines clearly, and, after it had completed a
sweeping circuit of the landing field, she could see the
lights of the low-flying Cessna coming in over the white
caps of the water. The roar of the engines grew proportionately as the plane taxied closer; they faded at
once to a dull whine when the power was cut and the
aircraft drew to a halt forty yards from where the cars
were parked.

A small red light winked on in the cabin. Samosa
hurriedly broke away from the other three men and
Megan saw Michael take a final drag from his cigar before dropping the butt onto the asphalt.

Gino was no longer lounging against the hood of the
car, but was standing erect and attentive, his eyes fixed
on the Cessna.

Megan wiped frantically at the mist her breath was
raising on the window. She could not shake her feel-

ings of apprehension and it suddenly became extremely important that she be able to hear and see everything clearly.

The hatched door of the Cessna popped open and a narrow flight of stairs was hydraulically lowered to the asphalt. Three men filed out of the plane, one of whom was greeted effusively by the bowing, grinning Samosa. After a brief exchange between the two men, they approached the line of cars, leaving the pair of guards behind, their automatic rifles very much in evidence.

"A safe flight, I presume?" Giancarlo asked. "Your pilot had no difficulty finding us?"

"He is a good man," the newcomer said. "You have the money? The agreed amount?"

Giancarlo grinned. "Ah, Mendoza—a true businessman, I see. Direct and to the point."

"I see no reason to linger any longer than necessary, do you?"

"None whatsoever. Michael?"

Michael nodded and walked around to the rear of the car. He opened the trunk and lifted two large metal suitcases, carrying them forward to where Gino had set up a portable, high-powered lamp. He set the cases on the car, spun the combinations on the locks, then opened them and stepped discreetly to one side.

"Ten million dollars was the amount agreed upon, I believe," said Giancarlo, inviting the man forward to inspect the contents of the cases. "Feel free to count it if you like."

Mendoza's eyes shone greedily as he stepped up to the car, but Giancarlo's hand intercepted him.

"After I see the plates, of course, and verify the quality of the merchandise I am buying."

The man withdrew an oblong leather box from the briefcase he was carrying and held it out to Giancarlo. Eagerly, the box was opened, revealing two felt-lined compartments divided and protected by a thick layer of foam.

"Naturally these will be less than ideal conditions for testing the workmanship, but you have my personal assurance the plates are perfect. The bills you strike from these—as you have seen from the sample we have provided—can pass all but the most intense microscopic scrutiny. With the proper materials and equipment, you can replace what you have here in the suitcases in a matter of a few weeks."

Megan dug her fingers into the upholstery of the seat in front of her, unaware she had leaned so far forward. *Plates!* Counterfeit plates for printing counterfeit money! While Hornsby had been chasing his tail in circles trying to gather evidence on Giancarlo's petty operations in Miami, Giancarlo had been setting his sights on a much higher goal.

And Michael had played a major part in it all.

She had become so engrossed with watching Giancarlo, she had actually forgotten about Michael. But he was there, standing with the others, peering over at Giancarlo while a test imprint of each plate was carefully made on the sheet of paper provided.

It was then that Megan made another startling discovery. Leaning forward as she was, she could see a glint of metal protruding from the steering column.

The key had been left in the ignition of the Mercedes!

The sight of it, although she was not quite sure what good it would do her, startled her heart into pounding again. The seats were high-backed and stationary, and by the time she could scramble over and settle herself in the driver's seat, she would have been noticed ten times over. Even so, it gave her something else to think about besides the glaringly obvious fact that she had just become inarguably expendable.

She was not naive; Giancarlo would not want to have an assistant district attorney as an eye witness to his purchase of counterfeit plates. He would want, if they were so assuredly perfect, to keep their existence a secret from the government for as long as possible. It was a secret that could be worth hundreds of millions of dollars to him—easily well worth the risk of an investigation into the "accidental" death of a vacationing attorney.

Megan concentrated on the key. She had to clamp her hands over her mouth to keep from crying out loud as the further realization came slamming home that Michael had been the one driving the Mercedes. Michael had left the key in the ignition. He had also left the window open, enabling her to hear as well as see everything that happened.

Before she could begin to make any sense of it, a movement from the group outside brought a gasp to her lips.

Michael had taken his gun from his jacket. He had stepped up behind Giancarlo and was thrusting the nose of the Beretta into Giancarlo's throat.

Giancarlo stiffened, his head still bent over the plates. No one else had seen the gun or the threat and their shock was complete as they heard Giancarlo's grunt of pain.

"If nobody makes any sudden moves, nobody gets hurt," Michael warned quietly.

Mendoza's hands froze on the stacks of money he was counting; Gino's instinctive reaction was to reach for the gun he wore concealed beneath his coat.

"Don't do it, Gino," Michael cautioned. "You and Vince would both be memories before you could get off a shot."

"Michael—" Giancarlo's hoarse whisper knifed through the silence "—*what the hell do you think you're doing?*"

"Taking care of a little unfinished business, Boss." He curled his forearm around the older man's neck and used the pressure of his gun to encourage Giancarlo to slowly straighten and accompany him away from the bulk of the car. "Mendoza, you can just slip those plates back into their case and lock them into one of the suitcases. Then you can slowly—slowly, I say—push the lot over here."

Giancarlo's face flushed red. "Michael, in God's name, why! Why are you doing this? You've been like a son to me. Haven't I treated you like my own flesh and blood?"

"Indeed you have. And wasn't I always as loyal and grateful as you expected me to be?"

"Then why—"

"I used to think it was because of the affection you had for my father, because you grew up together, because you were more like brothers than friends. That was why it was so hard for me to believe you were the one who ordered him killed."

"Killed!" Giancarlo tried to turn his head, and in the light, Megan saw fine beads of sweat forming on his forehead. "You don't know what you're talking about!"

"On the contrary. In the last few months I've come to know too damned much. Think back, Vince. You remember my brother Frank?"

"Frank? *Frank?* What does he have to do with this?"

"He went to prison to do time for someone you thought was more important in the scheme of things than a punk kid. He'd still be there today, rotting out a twenty-year term, if someone hadn't knifed him in his cell."

Giancarlo tried to swallow, but it was impossible. "Michael—"

The Beretta ground into the tender underside of Giancarlo's chin, finding and crushing his nerves to the point of agony.

"The warden said they had no idea who was responsible for Frank's death, but eventually, the money you spread around got a bit thin and a friend of his on the inside managed to get word out. Just a name, mind you. But the name belonged to the same man who was inside doing a life sentence for the murder of Nickolaus Antonacci. And do you know what else I found out? That same man was living the life of Riley...money, drugs, anything he wanted. You know why?"

Giancarlo gasped out an oath from between his purpling lips.

"Because he was serving his time under your protection, Vince. He was your man, bought and paid for. He did the hit on my father, and when it looked like my brother was closing in on the truth, he was ordered to take out Frank."

"No. No, Michael! I loved your father. We were *famiglia*. I would never do what you're accusing me of, not to your father, not to Frank."

"Not unless it was business and they stood in your way," Michael countered icily. "And my father did stand in your way, didn't he? He had the teamsters in the palm of his hand, and that gave him too much clout, too much power."

"Michael...we can talk about this. When we're calm and we have the chance to look at this carefully, we can talk about it."

"No. I've done all the talking I'm going to do...except maybe to Don Vannini. He doesn't know about this little transaction, does he? He doesn't know that one of his *capos* is getting greedy enough to think he can take over the entire family. These plates would have printed a lot of money, bought a lot of support for your takeover."

Giancarlo blinked at the sweat that was streaming into his eyes. He knew Michael too well to doubt his anger or his intentions.

So did Gino, whose low voice came from across the breadth of the car. "You won't get away with this, Mikey. Look around you. There are at least a dozen guns pointed at your heart."

"This is the only one that counts, though," Michael replied, gouging his gun deeper into Vincent's neck. "Now do what I asked you to do. Put the plates in the suitcase and push them over here."

To Megan, watching in horror from the darkness of the car, what happened next occurred in a terrifying kind of slow motion. She saw Gino move forward and place the counterfeit plates back in their nests of felt. He snapped the leather case shut and fit it on top of the stacks of bound bills in one of the suitcases. He leaned over to bring the lid of the suitcase down to close it, but with the case hiding his movements from Michael, he reached inside his jacket and drew his gun.

Michael responded to the flash of gunfire by swinging the snout of the Beretta away from Giancarlo's neck and discharging it at the more immediate threat. A second set of explosive flashes marked two more reports and this time both men staggered back—Gino careening in an arc backward to land heavily in the sand and weeds, and Michael spinning with the impact of the two hits and sprawling facedown on the tarmac.

In the next wild heartbeat, Megan's vision was shattered by a piercing white light. It came from everywhere and nowhere, surrounding and enveloping the cars and the airstrip, illuminating everyone under a brilliant wash of glaring floodlights.

At the same time, there were other explosions of gunfire. Long bursts of staccato rapid-fire came from the direction of the Cessna as the two guards sprayed blindly at the source of the lights. Simultaneously, the guards along the airstrip fired into the darkness, but their only response was from a deep, booming voice that came over a bullhorn.

"Lay your weapons down! This is the police! You are completely surrounded! Lay your weapons down at once!"

Vincent Giancarlo, his reflexes quick as a cat's grabbed for the suitcase containing the plates. He paused only the briefest fraction of a second to look down at Michael's body, at the spreading pool of blood beneath him, but it was a fraction of a second too long. Four men encased head to toe in black fatigues sprang out of the shadows, their automatic rifles pointed squarely at Giancarlo's chest.

The pilot of the Cessna booted his engines to full throttle, but there, too, he was seconds too late to avoid the searching beams of the pair of helicopters that swooped down out of the sky and blocked his escape along the runway.

Someone was screaming.

Megan covered her ears with her hands, but the screams stayed with her, reverberating around the airless interior of the car. She clawed at the car door, forgetting it was locked. She hammered on the windows with the heels of her hands, but no one paid her any attention. By then there were dozens of black-clad figures swarming around the cars, intent upon disarming and herding together Giancarlo and his gunmen.

A horribly familiar sound shrilled up the runway and the sight of the flashing red light caused Megan to fight for control, to help herself when no one else would. She leaned between the seats and managed to turn the key in the ignition. The controls for the power doors were located on a central panel and she stabbed every button she could see until she heard the solid metallic click of the locks releasing.

With a sob she pushed the door open and stumbled out of the car. There were men in white coats bending over Michael's prone body, and two more rushing between the cars to reach Gino Romani.

"Michael...!" Her cry was a whisper and her shock was such that she couldn't will her feet to move forward.

"What the hell—! Who's the woman?" The gravelly voice of authority belonged to a vague black shape that stepped in front of her and blocked her view. "Who the hell are you?"

"Please," she cried. "He's hurt. I have to go to him."

Rough, gnarled hands grasped her by the arm and prevented her from taking more than a couple of steps toward the medics working feverishly over Michael.

"Hold it, lady. You're not goin' anywhere until we know who you are and what you're doin' here tonight."

"Please! You don't understand!"

"Hell no, I don't understand, so why don't you start by tellin' me your name. You do have a name, don't you?"

Megan curled her icy-cold fingers into fists and pressed them against her lips. Michael was hurt, maybe dying, and they weren't going to let her see him or speak to him. Another dark shape crowded in on her, cutting across the path of bright light and pausing to show something to the man holding her before he dismissed him and took his place by Megan's side. The viselike grip of the first officer was replaced by the gentler grip of the second. His manner was soothing, and he spoke to her as he might to a daughter, or to a child in pain.

"He's just tryin' to do his job. Why don't you come on over here with me where we won't be in the way."

"I . . . have to help Michael," she cried.

"You'll only get in the doctor's way, and you wouldn't want to do that now, would you?"

Megan looked up at the officer's face, but the glare from the floodlights rendered the world nearly opaque through her tears, and she found herself focusing instead on the small identification badge he had flashed at the officer and was now clipping to his front breast pocket. His name—George Madison—along with a picture and identification number were encased in plastic, and typed across the top of the card in bold relief: POLICE.

15

MEGAN WAS TREMBLING, a shiver away from slipping into shock.

"Are you all right? You're not hurt, are you?"

"George?" she whispered. She dashed her hands across her eyes to clear them, yet still could not comprehend the reality that stood in front of her. It was George Samson. The same George Samson she had met in the rundown diner that first evening with Michael . . . only now his badge identified him as George Madison. Gone was the nonchalant air; in its place, a wiry toughness that attested to many years of experience. Gone as well was the drawled Bahamian accent along with the ragged clothing and the grayed stubble of beard.

"George?" she asked again, more bewildered than ever. "What is going on? Where did all these men come from? Where did *you* come from?"

The expression on his wizened face betrayed his genuine reluctance to be the one answering her questions. He wasn't sure how much she knew or how much he should assume she wanted to know. Moreover, he was in no mood to match wits with the shimmering pool of tears standing in her eyes. He almost hadn't recognized her as the slim and elegant, perfectly manicured beauty Vallaincourt had brought to the diner. Her hair had sprung loose from the hasty ponytail she had made. Her face was smudged and her clothes bulky and shape-less.

"Look, why don't you let me take you back to one of the vans. They'll have blankets and coffee—"

"I don't want coffee. I want to know what happened here tonight! I want to see Michael!"

"No," he said firmly. "You don't. Now you stay put. Right here. Move or try to interfere in any way and I won't ask you if you want to go back in one of the vans, I'll have you put there bodily. You understand me?"

Megan trembled with anger with confusion, with a painful desperation to know what was happening on the tarmac, but she nodded. "I . . . won't interfere."

"Good." George signaled to another officer stand-ing nearby. "She wasn't any part of this, not voluntar-ily anyway, but you had best get some kind of statement for the report. Okay, folks—" he raised his voice and started walking toward the hub of activity "—radio the vans to come in and let's start shipping these pretty boys back to headquarters. Keep 'em separated, though. We don't want too many stories sounding too much alike. Well, well, well, what do we have here?"

He stopped and leaned over the opened suitcases. The bundled stacks of money earned a cursory glance, but it was the plates that caused his lips to purse around a low whistle.

Lifting one of them carefully out of its felt bed to ex-amine it more closely, George cocked an eyebrow in Giancarlo's direction.

"I guess this explains why you'd be wanting to give this particular transaction your personal attention. Real beauties, ain't they? Mendoza does some good work down there in Brazil. Pity he's been doing it under the watchful eyes of one of our own fine apprentices."

Giancarlo's hands were cuffed, but the clenched fists were a satisfying clue that George's sarcasm had not gone unappreciated.

George glanced sidelong at the bloodstained sheet that had been drawn over Gino Romani's body, then at the sudden lack of activity surrounding the other body on the tarmac.

"I don't suppose you'd care to elaborate on what happened here, would you?"

Giancarlo glared. "Why don't you ask them."

George grimaced as the doctors began removing the tubes and collecting up the bags of fluids and dressings that would no longer be required. He caught one intern's eye and saw him shake his head over Michael's body—a gesture that was not lost on Giancarlo.

"Revenge, my friend," George said distastefully. "A pretty powerful incentive. You must have really done something to piss him off—Vallaincourt was his name, wasn't it?"

Giancarlo spat an oath and turned his head away.

"Gee—don't go gettin' all maudlin on me, Mr. Giancarlo. It spoils the mood of the celebration."

"You had better celebrate while you can, old man, because these—" he held up his manacled wrists and snorted derisively "—will be off before you can finish your paperwork."

George smiled. "I wouldn't go counting up my bail money just yet if I was you. In the first place, you've got enough ink on your hands to do most of the paper-

work for us, never mind giving our print man a re-
warding night's work matching thumbs and forefingers
and pinkies. Very sloppy, Vince. You're going to be a lot
older than me before your lawyers can figure a way out
of this one—that's assuming you want them to get you
out once Carlos Vannini hears what you've been up to.
Tsk, tsk tsk. He may be old, but he's still plenty feisty."

Giancarlo scowled and muttered a string of invec-
tives in Italian.

"Yeah, well, I'm sure that goes for your mother, as
well." George waved at one of his men. "Get this piece
of garbage out of here."

When the last of the vehicles had been loaded and
were rolling away along the gravel road, George gave
the high sign to cut some of the floodlights. He paused
by the ambulance to talk to the doctors, then knelt beside Michael's body. He shook his head once, twice,
then ran his gnarled fingers over the dome of his head.

Frowning, the steps that carried him back to where
Megan waited were paced to the thoughts dragging on
his mind. Megan had an untouched cup of coffee
steaming in her hands and a woolen blanket draped
loosely over her shoulders.

"I should have retired from this job years ago," he
muttered. "No more ulcers. No more phone calls gettin' me out of a warm bed at two o'clock in the morning. No more *crap*."

He squinted up at Megan's face and was obviously
not too thrilled about what he had come to say. She
braced herself for the worst. She was far too numb to
cry, still too deep in shock to even begin to sort out what

had happened. Michael had loved her, then betrayed her, but in the end . . .

"He tried to help me," she said in a low voice. "He left the keys in the car so I would be able to get away in all the confusion. Do you think that meant . . . ?"

That he loved her? Or, if love was too strong a word to use, did it mean that he cared? Even if it was just a little, just at the end? She didn't know if it would make hearing George's news any easier to bear.

Megan had also seen the doctors moving away from Michael's body and she did not need to see George's face for confirmation. Michael was dead. The man she loved . . . hated . . . loved, was dead, and she was alone again. All her confusion, her endless agonizing over what was right and what was wrong . . . it had all been for nothing. A waste. She could feel proud of herself that she had not compromised her position of her vaunted principles . . . but Michael was dead and she was alone, so how much further ahead was she for all her moral outrage?

"Where did we both go wrong?" she wondered aloud.

George scratched his head and muttered something under his breath. "Look, Miss Worth, I don't agree this is the right thing to do, but it doesn't look like he's leaving me much choice. I can give you five minutes with him, no more. We gotta get him off the island before anyone comes sniffin' around, asking too many questions."

"I don't . . . understand."

George stepped aside so that Megan had a clear view of the area in front of the ambulance. Michael's body was no longer stretched out on the asphalt. The doctors were there, laughing over some shared anecdote, but their patient was gone.

"Michael...?"

She caught a slight movement out of the corner of her eye and turned to stare uncomprehendingly at the two men who were emerging from the shadows behind the Mercedes. Michael slowed, then stopped. Gino Romani finished untaping the sprung bladder of fake blood from beneath his shirt and stopped, as well.

The blanket slipped from Megan's shoulders and fell unnoticed onto the ground. The coffee cup followed, landing with a clatter of plastic and splashed liquid. She pressed her hands over her mouth and was aware of the air rasping hotly along a throat that was already raw and dry.

Gino exchanged a sheepish look with Michael before moving quickly away to join George well back of the floodlit asphalt.

Michael took an awkward step closer, then another. "I'm sorry. It was the only way."

Megan stared. At the wave of blue-black hair that blew forward over his forehead and was thrust away by an impatient hand. At the gory red mess that soaked through the front of his white shirt and still dripped in a slow *pat pat pat* on the ground.

Michael followed her gaze and swore. "I told them it had to look convincing, I didn't know they would make it look like a replay of *The Wild Bunch*."

Megan blinked, then looked up in disbelief. "You're ... not hurt?"

"No." He ripped his shirt open to show her that he had been rigged with the same kind of explosive sacks as Gino had been wearing. "The bullets were blanks, but we needed more than a lot of noise and confusion to make Vince believe we were dead."

His ready smile faded when there was no immediate response to his confession, and he took another cautious step closer, a frown creasing his handsome face.

"If it's any consolation, I gave my head a pretty good crack when I hit the pavement."

Megan's attention was drawn reluctantly to the serrated lump that was swelling on his temple. It was blue and looked painful. She also saw the tautly corded veins standing out on his neck, throbbing with the apprehension that coursed through his body. There was something else—something in his eyes that caused her to shiver involuntarily, and kept her from turning on her heels and walking away from him. Those twin impenetrable windows to his heart and soul were not as unreadable as he hoped they were, or perhaps thought they would be in the eerie blue-white spill of the floodlights. There was fear shadowing their depths—a genuine fear of her anger and her rejection.

With good reason.

"What would you have done if they had started shooting at you with real bullets?" she asked in amazement.

"I would have blamed it on Gino. It was his idea in the first place."

"*His* idea?"

Michael nodded. "He and George both. They set the whole thing up after they found out Giancarlo had commissioned the counterfeit plates from Mendoza. They figured they could do it better if they had someone on the inside, someone Vince trusted.

"They came to me a few months ago with the information about my brother's death. Naturally, I was all for killing Vince outright and taking my chances afterward, but Gino convinced me there was a better way."

"This?" Megan asked, spreading her hand to indicate the chaos on the airstrip.

"It suited both our purposes. George—like your agent Hornsby—has been trying to pin something on Giancarlo for a long time. When he heard about the plates, he knew it would be important enough for Vince to handle personally. More so when he saw how perfect the counterfeit hundreds were."

"The night at the diner," she said slowly. "I thought you paid an exorbitant amount of money for a few pots of seafood."

"I must be slipping," he said, frowning. "I didn't think you'd noticed. Either that, or I wasn't thinking at all—at least not with my head."

A twinge of indignation sent Megan's eyebrows arching upward. "And you apparently didn't think much of *my* powers of reasoning. Did it never occur to you that a few days of sex and sunshine would hardly make me go blind, deaf, or dumb? Couldn't you have trusted me?"

"You asked me very specifically not to lie to you," he said quietly. "The truth wasn't safe for you to know, so I had to tell you as little as possible."

Their eyes met and locked and there was a breathless little silence between them as they both pondered the mistakes and misunderstandings.

"I thought you were dead," she said softly. "I was standing here feeling sorry for myself, feeling cheated and betrayed and...and sorry for *you* because you had died without knowing..." Words failed her for a moment and she had to look away, to break the terrible hold of his eyes. When she looked back, she could almost ignore the effect of the lights on his profile, or the distinctive scent of his wretched little cigars that came to her on the breeze.

"You are a very good actor, Michael. You've been convincing in both the roles you've played. All three, if you want to add this minor movie audition to your résumé. What I'm wondering is, am I about to see a fourth?"

"Megan—"

"Because if I am, I'd rather pass. I don't think I could bear any more pain tonight."

Michael nodded slowly. "I deserve that. I deserve it and I don't blame you one bit for feeling the way you do. It wasn't fair to put you through any of this."

"No. It wasn't."

"I suppose...it could have something to do with the Italian side of me."

"*What?*"

"The Italian blood flows from the neck up, the French from the neck down. Unfortunately, it's the Italian influence that tends to make a man think sometimes... well..."

"That he's the man and the woman is the woman and should know her rightful place in the greater scheme of things? My God, how archaic."

"I didn't say I felt that way. And I never, for a moment, actually believed it."

"I'm glad you didn't," she said through her teeth. "It would have made the prospect of giving you another crack on the head too appealing to resist."

Michael looked startled, then relieved, and the relief was so genuine, she had to fight hard not to respond to his smile.

"So what happens now?" she asked crisply.

"Now . . . hopefully Mr. Vincent Giancarlo spends a very long time behind bars. Because he was caught red-handed with the goods, my involvement—voluntary or otherwise—ends right here and I walk away a relatively free man."

"Relatively?"

"I never agreed to do more than give them Giancarlo. As long as I keep it that way and avoid showing my face in any highly populated areas, I shouldn't have to look over my shoulder every time I hear a car backfire. Nevertheless, there is always the possibility I could be recognized somewhere down the road, something I guess I'll have to deal with when and if it happens."

She did not want to delve further into the implications of what he said, and instead, let her gaze drift down to the crimson stains on his shirt.

"When . . . did you do all this?"

"After I left the bungalow. I was supposed to go and find Dallas—which I did, you might be relieved to know, and told him, in turn, to release your cousin as soon as it was safe to do so."

Megan's eyes narrowed. "Did you know Giancarlo would be waiting for me in my room?"

Cornered again, he avoided the question briefly, turning into the light so that his lean features were silhouetted in profile. After a moment, he sighed, raked his fingers through the shaggy main of his hair.

"Gino came to warn me that Vince was there, waiting for both of us. He had figured out who you were, but he didn't know why you were here and he didn't like the fact that I had kept the information from him. I wanted to go after you and stop you before you got to your room, but that only would have made Vince more suspicious. Gino . . . and I . . . thought you could handle yourself. And you did."

"Handle myself? I was frightened half to death. And Shari? God only knows how terrified she was by all this."

Michael took a halting step forward, but caught himself and stopped. "Don't you see, I had no choice, Megan. I had to play along with him, and I had to let you think I was a bastard so that nothing you said or did would let him see how much you meant to me. I never for a moment thought he would bring you along tonight. Hell, I had no idea if we could even pull this off, let alone do it and come out in one piece. And if something went wrong, whether Vince was caught or not, jailed or not, he would have lashed out at anything or anyone he thought was important to me. I couldn't take that chance, Megan. I had to make him think you meant nothing to me, and for that to happen, your hatred for me had to be real."

"It was," she said quietly. "I couldn't believe you had lied to me . . . lied to me about everything."

Michael dragged his eyes away from hers with an effort. "I may have avoided telling you the truth about a few things over the past week, but I never lied about my feelings for you. And tonight? Tonight I was a bastard but I had to know you would be safe when this was over. I had to guarantee you wouldn't become a target, even if it meant losing you. I still want you to be safe," he added pointedly.

All the anger and resentment drained from Megan's heart as she suddenly realized what he was saying. Nothing had changed. He was still going to walk out of her life, leaving her alone.

"But . . . I don't want to lose you, Michael. Not like this. Not when there isn't any reason why we can't be together."

Michael bowed his head and she could see a fine mist of salt spray clinging to the jet-black waves.

"You have your career, your life ahead of you, that's reason enough. I could never ask you to give any part of it up for me." He looked up and his expression was oddly calm, unexpectedly composed. "In fact, if you play your cards right, you can take most of the credit for what happened here tonight. With the publicity and the kudos for putting Giancarlo behind bars, there is no reason why you can't go all the way to the top of the heap."

"What if I said I don't want to go to the top? What if I said it doesn't mean anything to me anymore, that none of it means anything to me without you?"

Michael smiled sadly. "I'd have to say you weren't thinking too clearly yet, that you were still in shock."

"My thinking is perfectly clear, and if I'm in shock, it's because you still seem to think my love for you isn't every bit as strong, as important as yours is for me. It is very noble of you, Michael, to offer to sacrifice yourself for my career, but it isn't going to work. What's more, it isn't a sacrifice I'm prepared to accept."

Michael reached out and gently touched her cheek. For just a moment, she thought she might actually have won, but in the next, she saw the closed expression take hold of his features again and force his emotions aside.

"So now who is being noble?" he murmured.

Megan grasped his wrist, holding his hand against her cheek when he would have taken it away.

"I'm not being noble, damn you. I told you earlier that I would do anything you asked me to do. I didn't realize what 'anything' meant until I saw you lying there on the tarmac. I love you, Michael. It isn't something that's going to go away, or be forgotten, or something I can bury in a career. I'm fairly successful at what I do, yes, and in time I could probably become exactly what my family wants me to become—a cold, lonely woman, dried up on the inside, hard and uncompromising on the outside. That's the life you're condemning me to, Michael. That's the future you're too proud to ask me to give up."

The smoldering blue-gray eyes fastened almost desperately on hers. She felt the tremor in his hand and she sensed the battle being waged between his logic and his emotions. It raged longer than she thought she could bear, and, with a fierce gasp of frustration, she ran her hands up and around his shoulders, lacing her fingers tight and slanting his face down to within an inch of hers.

"Tell me you don't love me," she said flatly. "Tell me you want me to walk out of your life forever, and I'll go."

A muscle shivered in his jaw. "If you had any sense at all, you wouldn't walk away from me, you'd run."

"Then tell me to go. Tell me you'll be happier on your own. Tell me you won't miss me, and you won't think of me, and you won't ever feel bad about breaking the only real promise you ever made me."

He frowned and stared at the lushness of her lips. "What promise?"

"The one about every minute of every hour of every day until we're both too weak to stand."

His eyes rose slowly to hers. She pressed her body closer to his and felt the heat of her name leave his lips on a gritty whisper.

"I have nothing to offer you. I don't even know where I'm going."

"We can find a place together. Somewhere small and private, where I can play on the beach and watch you terrorize the gulls on your Harley."

"It sounds boring," he declared, but his hands were weakening, circling slowly around her waist.

"It sounds heavenly," she whispered. "We'll throw away our clothes, and you can teach me how to fish…"

She felt his smile as she pressed her lips against his, and she heard his throaty laugh as his mouth claimed hers with a power and a passion that swept away any doubts lingering in her mind. His arms tightened, holding her with a hunger that caused her body to burst into flames everywhere they touched.

"Michael...? Um, excuse me... Michael?"

Neither had been aware of George Madison moving into their floodlit arena, or of the genuinely pained expression on his face as he observed the two lovers embracing.

He cleared his throat and called again, and this time Michael released her mouth, but remained boldly, adamantly locked against her body.

"The chopper is waiting, Michael. You'd better be on your way."

The blazing blue eyes did not leave Megan's face. "Is there room for another passenger?"

Megan's heart sang with joy and she reached hungrily for his lips again.

George gaped at the two of them as if they had lost their minds. "What? What did you just say?"

Michael freed his mouth with difficulty. "You heard me. The lady is coming along."

George yanked a recently lit cigar out of his mouth and dashed it to the ground. "Are you crazy? What do you think we're running here, a taxi service? I told you this was a bad idea. I told you it would be better to leave well enough alone, but no. No, you had to talk to her. You just had to talk to her. D'you know what you're doin', man? Do either one of you know what you're doin?"

"We have a rough idea," Michael said easily. "But then you're already married, George, so why don't you tell us what we're getting into."

"Married?" George's eyes popped out of their creases. "Did you say married?"

"I did indeed . . . if she'll have me."

George groaned and turned to Gino in the hope of enlisting the cool voice of reason. But Gino had a dilemma of his own to solve—a dilemma that was pulling to a screeching halt in a spray of dust and gravel; a dilemma with short, curly red hair who threw herself out of the car and left Dallas to figure out how to shift the Ferrari into park.

"I don't believe it," George muttered. "It's a circus. I got me a damned circus!"

Michael turned back to Megan, ignoring George's theatrics as the senior agent launched into a long litany of protests and threats.

"Well?" he asked softly. "Will you marry me, Megan Worth?"

Her eyes shining, she leaned her head against his shoulder. "Only if it's forever."

Michael smiled. "Forever probably won't be long enough, but we'll give it a try, shall we?"

HARLEQUIN Temptation

Rebels & Rogues

All men are not created equal. Some are rough around the edges. Tough-minded but tenderhearted. Incredibly sexy. The tempting fulfillment of every woman's fantasy.

When it's time to fight for what they believe in, to win that special woman, our Rebels and Rogues are heroes at heart. Twelve Rebels and Rogues, one each month in 1992, only at Temptation!

Jake: He was a rebel with a cause, but a beautiful woman threatened it all.

THE WOLF by Madeline Harper.
Temptation #389, April.

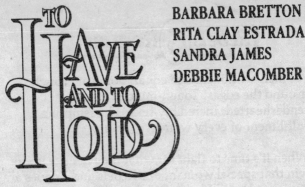